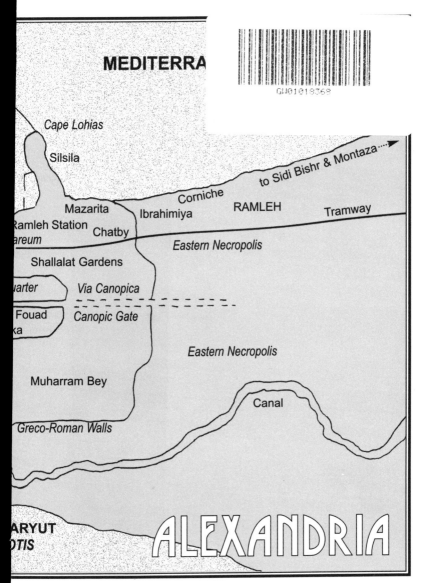

MEDITERRA

Cape Lohias

Silsila

to Sidi Bishr & Montaza·····

Corniche

Mazarita Ibrahimiya RAMLEH Tramway

amleh Station Chatby
areum

Eastern Necropolis

Shallalat Gardens

uarter *Via Canopica*

Fouad *Canopic Gate*
a

Eastern Necropolis

Muharram Bey

Canal

Greco-Roman Walls

ARYUT
TIS

ALEXANDRIA

Buildings and Landmarks of
Ancient Alexandria
and
Modern Alexandria

Farewell
to
Alexandria

Farewell
to
Alexandria

Eleven Short Stories by
Harry E. Tzalas

Translated by
Susan E. Mantouvalou

Illustrated by
Anna Boghiguian

The American University in Cairo Press

The American University in Cairo Press
113 Sharia Kasr el Aini
Cairo, Egypt
http://aucpress.com

Dar el Kutub No. 14350/99
ISBN 977 424 555 5

Printed in Egypt by Elias Modern Press

Contents

Prologue

The eleven narratives contained in this book were written at different times. The first, *Osta Antoun*, was written at the end of the 1970s, the last, *The Quails*, fifteen years later.

Osta Antoun, *The Little Armenian Girl*, *The Maestro*, and *Frau Grete* were all written before my visit to Alexandria in the spring of 1988—the first time I had revisited the city since my emigration in 1956.

Much of *Amm Ahmad, Father and Son* was jotted down in a school exercise-book during that brief visit to the city in 1988 and completed later, upon my return to Athens.

These stories were followed by *Athinodoros and Iordanis*; *Sidi Bishr, October 1942*; *The Three Brothers*; *Alexandrea ad Aegyptum*; *The As and the Fs of History*; and the collection was completed with *The Quails*.

I feel the need to write these few lines to explain the difference in style that the reader will find in narratives that were written many years apart. I never seriously thought of rewriting, altering, or correcting the originals. It would seem, somehow, to devalue them. I should also add that the heroes of these stories are real people who lived in Alexandria; they are as real as the city itself.

Alexandria—the last great cosmopolitan center of the Mediterranean—is special, unique, because people of different nationalities and faiths lived there, people going about their ordinary, everyday lives. They lived side by side—Muslims, Copts, Nubians, Greeks, Italians, Armenians, Maltese, Shamis, Lebanese, Jews, English, French, Spaniards,

Germans, Austrians—they were all Alexandrians; together they made up the whole. They laid the foundations of the new Alexandria upon the remains of the ancient city.

Many famous people have lived in Alexandria—people like Constantine Cavafy, Giuseppe Ungaretti, Fausta Cialente, E.M. Foster, Lawrence Durrell, Stratis Tsirkas—but it is not because of them that Alexandria is special. It is special because of the everyday people who were born and raised there—Amm Ahmad, Frau Grete, Osta Antoun and the Maestro, Docteur Tawa and the little Armenian girl from next door, the Jew Vivante, Frère Jean-Baptiste, Athinodoros and Iordanis, Badri with his three wives and umpteen children.

These are the true Alexandrians, and it is to them that we owe a debt.

Farewell
to
Alexandria

Osta Antoun

Antoun was a poor Lebanese shoemaker, born in Alexandria, as was his father, and his father before him. He spoke Arabic as well as French. He was a Christian and dressed in the European fashion, not in a *gallabiya* like the locals. Which of his forefathers had first come to Egypt from Lebanon and just when they settled in Alexandria Antoun did not know, but then, such questions did not concern him.

Antoun was a master shoemaker. After years of apprenticeship as assistant to a master craftsman, he himself became a master and had his own assistant. He was worthy of the Arabic title *osta*, master craftsman. He worked in a cobbler's workshop owned by an Armenian, and he was respectfully known as 'Osta Antoun.'

I remember the last time I saw him as if it were only yesterday, and yet over forty years have passed since then. He was tall, gangly, middle-aged, with sparse, graying hair, which he wore flattened against his temples. He pestered the little hair he had, combing it this way and that in a futile effort to cover up his baldness. He had a sunburned face, a large, crooked nose, black, eagle eyes with a steady gaze like an iron spear, and a jet-black, short-trimmed mustache that he tended with care and dyed regularly.

Osta Antoun was poor, poor as can be, with a wage of just ten pounds a month. His eldest daughter had to go out to work so that they could make ends meet. Things were difficult. How was he supposed to keep his family on so little? He toiled all day at the Armenian's workshop and in the evenings he took on other work at home. That was done secretly, because if his boss had found out about it, Antoun would have been fired.

He took home a few leftover pieces of leather one day, another day a sole or two, a heel, a little wax, a few nails. With these materials he made two or three pairs of shoes a month, working all through the night in his paltry apartment.

In those days shoes were made by hand. There were no presses, no machines. Shoes were heavy, stiff. They hurt your heels for a month or two until you broke them in, until the leather had softened, but then they would last for many years.

Antoun kept the money he earned from his nighttime work aside and spent it on his only pastime—fishing. He handed all his wages over to his wife, but his nighttime earnings were his pocket money. Of course, Madame Angele complained and grumbled about this great extravagance, but Antoun was adamant. "I haven't any other indulgences in life," he said. "I don't smoke, I don't play backgammon, I never go to the café or the cinema."

On Sundays, come rain or shine, he would get up eagerly before daybreak to go fishing. It was dark. The city was asleep. Not a soul on the streets. Only the occasional weak, trembling light of an oil lamp from the corner of an alley.

From the distant, poor neighborhood where he lived, Antoun crossed the city on foot until he came to the café where the fishermen gathered to wait for the dawn and for the bait—small, live shrimp—to arrive.

So on Sundays Osta Antoun would become a new man. We could hear him approaching from way off; his heavy boots with their small metal tips echoed on the cobbled street. Click, click, click. And then a thin, dark figure would appear out of the dim, hazy mist, a long stick over one shoulder— his fishing rods in their case—and a large wicker basket in his left hand. When I first saw him I was afraid. I was still a

small boy then and I said to myself, "He must be the bogey-man my mother says will come to take me away if I don't eat up all my food."

Antoun had at least ten fishing rods, and depending upon the season and the spot where he was fishing he would choose the appropriate one: a small, thin rod for the little fish; a short, sturdy, Indian rod for the big ones. He was a good fisherman. He loved his rods and gave each of them a name. His favorite was called Mahrusa; a fine, lithe, svelte, Indian rod that whistled like a whip when he cast his line. He had named her after Farouk's royal yacht.

•

Just like every man on this earth, Antoun had an unfulfilled desire, a longing; he yearned for that which would make his life more comfortable, his Sundays more pleasant.

Do not imagine that Antoun entertained any frivolous desires. He was a simple, down-to-earth man with simple, down-to-earth needs and modest dreams: Antoun wanted a watch.

He did not have a timepiece—no clock at home, no watch in his pocket, and no watch on his wrist. I have no idea how he managed to regulate his life. Of course, the call of the muezzin from the high minaret helped, calling Allah's faithful to prayer at regular intervals. But Antoun missed not having a watch.

In the café on Sunday mornings when daybreak came, his first words would be, "What time is it?" Then he would say good morning to everyone and begin talking about the fish he had caught last Sunday, about the one that got away—that huge black fish, the one that fought for a whole hour before the line snapped and he made off.

By the time they had drunk their coffee, the shrimp man would arrive with his mass of minuscule, diaphanous prawns wriggling in big baskets, glistening like the rain. What a crush! Everyone pushed and shoved to be first to get the bait, because the shrimp man, a cunning Copt, put the live bait on top, with the old, stale bait underneath for the latecomers.

As soon as they had their bait, the fishermen set off in small groups. Some walked to the nearby coast, the Corniche as we called it; some went as far as the headland of the ancient Cape Lochias, Silsila, at the tip of the Eastern Harbor. Others took the first tram of the day heading for the coal stores at the port to take a fishing boat from there. There were so many fishing grounds in Alexandria, and everywhere there were fish, so many fish!

Even though he was talkative beforehand, as soon as the fishing began Antoun fell silent. You could not get a word out of him when he was fishing and he would not allow anybody near him to speak. I was a little afraid of him, ever since the time I got my feet tangled up in his fishing line and he shot me a cold look with those tiny eyes of his which I thought would fling me into the sea. He could be bad-tempered, but deep down he was a good man.

He set up his small stool at the edge of the pier and sat with care. He began to prepare his tackle. He plumbed his line, checked the cork and skillfully baited his hook. Whoosh! There was a sharp swishing sound as he flicked back his rod and cast hook, line, and sinker into the sea.

Then he would fix his eyes upon the cork float, almost holding his breath, waiting patiently for the fish to bite, for the float to bob, to sink a little. At the first bite, the fish would timidly test the bait, and then would suddenly snatch at it and head for deeper water. The float would disappear. With one sharp yank on his rod Antoun would hook the fish and the silent struggle between the fish and the fisherman would begin.

The fisherman nearly always won.

•

Slowly the sun would begin to rise. In the summer, when it

got hot, Antoun would put on a straw hat and carry on with his fishing. He enjoyed every minute. Occasionally he would ask the fisherman next to him, "What time is it?" He said this very quietly, almost in a whisper, as if he were afraid that the fish would hear him.

And so the day would pass.

In the afternoon, when the fish were no longer biting, the fishermen packed up their tackle with slow, unhurried movements, and then began to walk leisurely back home.

Antoun would find his tongue and his heartiness again. He rarely returned home with his wicker basket empty. He generally caught plenty of fish, and when he did he fairly glowed with joy, gesticulating as he talked and laughing a great deal.

They were happy at home too. The girls ran to meet him— Madame Angele too—to empty his basket, to touch the fish, to count them, to admire them.

All week long, from Monday to Saturday, life was routine, the days as identical as carbon copies. But Sundays were different; they were filled with a thousand little thrills brought by the fishing.

From time to time, Ismail, a fellow cobbler and also a fisherman, would complain about the job. "Long hours, poor pay."

Ismail was a grumbler. Antoun could not stand it. He never complained, he was resigned to his fate. For him there were poor folk and rich folk and between the two an insurmountable wall. He was on the poor side; he found this natural, he did not make comparisons. He could not imagine himself being in any other position.

Now, thanks to the union—yes, the cobblers had a trade union—they no longer worked on Sundays.

"Do you remember, Ismail?" shouted Antoun. "Back before the war, when we worked a half-day on Sundays?" He shuddered just to remember those years. They used to get just one day's holiday a year—the day of Shamm al-Nesim, the Orthodox Easter Monday. They worked every Sunday until two in the afternoon. They even worked half a day on Easter Sunday and on Christmas Day and New Year's Day. This applied not only to the shoemakers, but to all the working class. But now the union had managed, with great difficulty and after endless negotiations, to secure them a whole day off per week, a day when you could do whatever you pleased, and this ingrate Ismail, this revolutionary, was not even satisfied. He wanted more. What? To be paid without working? Antoun crossed himself.

"May God protect the boss," he said. "May he gather great wealth so that we might have a slice of bread to eat."

During the summer, Sundays did not end with the fishing. After he had eaten, Antoun would take a nap, and in the evening the whole family would go out. They would stroll down to Ramleh Station, the two girls in front, Antoun and his wife behind. They would mingle with the cosmopolitan crowds. They would saunter around looking in the shop windows and at the photographs outside the cinemas; they would pass outside the large pastry shops, Athenaios, Baudrot, Pastroudis', Tornazakis'. Hungrily they would inhale the warm aroma that filled the air from the cakes being baked in the basement pastry kitchens.

Then Antoun would say, "Come on, girls, my treat," and he would buy them an ice cream cornet or a pitta bread filled with warm, delicious *fuul*.

•

One day, a letter arrived to disturb the peaceful waters of Antoun's life. An uncle of his in Beirut had died. Antoun had forgotten all about him.

Uncle Michel had lived all his life in Beirut. He had a shop selling leather pelts, and he was quite well-to-do. Every two or three years he would visit Alexandria for a month in the summer. Now Uncle Michel had died, and he had remembered Antoun in his will, leaving him a small plot of land.

Antoun could not believe it. He kept saying so again and again—it was too good to be true.

He would sell the land and start his own business, open a shoe shop. But he had no idea how much that would cost. He kept asking the lawyer, calculating, making hypothetical plans. Gone were those carefree Sundays! He still went fishing, of course, but how was he supposed to concentrate on the fish? He talked all the while about what he would do with the income from the piece of land; he dreamed. Where would he set up the shoe shop? He asked for other people's opinions, proposed partnerships. Other times he would change his mind; he said he would start a workshop to make soap. Yes, perfumed soap.

Every Sunday, as before, he would go to the café where the fishermen gathered at daybreak. After asking, "What time is it?" he would say a hurried good morning. He would order his coffee and would begin to complain. "The money hasn't arrived yet, but it won't be long now, the lawyer said so."

•

Three years passed like this, three years full of anguish, dreams, calculations; three years full of shoes and perfumed soap. Osta Antoun's tiny perfumed bars of soap permeated my childhood imagination. I could see them just as he described them: smooth, round, and colored—pink, blue, green, and lavender—and how beautifully they smelled of jasmine and *full*, like the garlands the little boys sold on Sunday evenings on Ramleh Boulevard.

As the time drew nearer for him to come into his inheritance, Antoun became more and more restless.

Then one day, the money arrived. When the expenses had been deducted, there were just two hundred pounds left. That was a lot of money for Antoun—almost two years' wages.

But the joy of the first day gave way to feelings of doubt that tortured poor Antoun. Should he start his own business—should he open the shoe shop or the little soap factory? Perhaps he should listen to the advice of Artin, his coworker, who said he should put the money in the bank.

And what sort of business could you start with two hundred pounds, anyway? He would have to borrow more. For a week, for ten days, Antoun could not make up his mind. He could not sleep, he lost his appetite, he was moody, and that Sunday he did not even go fishing. He stayed at home. He did not get out of bed. He was thinking. A great struggle was going on inside him. He had nightmares.

The next day he got up very early. He had made his decision. He put the two hundred pounds into his pocket and went to a watchmaker's on Rue Fouad. He bought a nice wall clock for the house, a pendulum clock that chimed on the hour and the half-hour. He bought a pocketwatch with a long chain for himself. For his wife, a wristwatch with eighteen rubies, a beautiful thing. He did not want his daughters to feel left out, so he got them each a watch too. There were a few pounds left over, so he bought a small radio. It was a Pye, English—Antoun had great faith in English products and boundless respect for Great Britain.

And so the two hundred pounds were spent and Antoun once again found peace.

On Sundays when he reached the café, he no longer asked what time it was. He said good morning and sat down at the wobbly table in the corner, ordered his coffee, and proudly drew his watch with its silver chain out of his pocket.

So Antoun did not start his own business, he never became a boss himself, but he had risen to the ranks of those who have a watch. And that was enough for him.

•

The years passed. I left Alexandria. Osta Antoun died. I got the news when I met an old acquaintance who used to go fishing with us on Sundays.

"Antoun passed on," he said. "May God have mercy on his

soul. He was a good man. It was his heart, you know. He was buried holding his watch tightly in his hands."

The Little Armenian Girl

It was in all the papers. The photograph made the front page. The *Pobeda* was coming: a great, white Russian ship to carry the Armenians back home.

The arrival of a Russian ship so soon after the war was quite an event. All the Europeans of Alexandria were talking about it. The *Pobeda* was to take the first of the repatriating Armenians, and other ships would follow for the rest.

There was a large Armenian community in Alexandria that had its own schools, churches, sporting clubs, fraternities, folk-dancing groups. The Armenians were quiet, hard-working people—money-changers, jewelers, tradesmen, cobblers, small businessmen. They lived peaceably in the European parts of the city, alongside the Greeks and the Italians, the Jews and the Maltese. They were enterprising stalwarts of the great cosmopolitan Alexandria, and yet they preserved the language, religion, traditions, and customs of their forefathers.

The ancient Armenian race had known fortune and fame, but had fallen on hard times. They had been victimized and hunted until they found themselves scattered all over the globe. Many had come to settle in Egypt. But just as they were beginning to put down roots, just as those who had been the first to arrive, old men now, sat back to admire the grandchildren who had been born in the welcoming land of the Ptolemies, it was time for them to move on again, to pack up once more. Those who could, went to their relatives in affluent countries like America, Canada, and France.

Dikran, my classmate, was the son of a cobbler. A shy, chubby lad, he left with his family for Canada. Artin, who ran the little corner shop just down the road, stocked with every imaginable merchandise—right down to silkworms—left for Marseilles, where he had a well-to-do cousin. Those who had no one to invite them to some foreign land accepted the invitation of Soviet Armenia to return to their homeland, or what was left of it outside Turkish rule.

Bogos, the tailor's son, said, "We're going to Yerevan. You can see Mount Ararat from there."

I had heard of Mount Ararat in scripture classes. It was on the high peak of that mountain, they said, that Noah's Ark had come to rest.

"My God," I thought. "What on earth is Bogos going to do on such high snowy peaks?"

•

Who knows how many generations had passed since the Armenians had come to Alexandria. I asked Dikran, but he had no idea.

"Ask your grandfather," I suggested. "He's sure to know."

Old Karabet, who was blind in one eye, told him that the Armenians had arrived before the great massacre by the Turks.

"How evil those Turks must be," I reflected. My grandmother, the Chiot, was not fond of them either. She called them "cruel barbarians."

Whenever I heard of slaughter and barbaric acts, it always brought to mind what my mother had told me, something she had heard from her mother before her, about the revolution of Urabi Pasha. They said that the Egyptians had risen up and slaughtered many Europeans in Alexandria. That disaster took place in 1882. As happens so often throughout history, the uprising of a genuine patriot who could no longer bear to watch his nation being oppressed by an abusive leadership and humbled by foreign powers—in this case

England and France—degenerated into frenzied plundering and the slaughter of innocents. It seems this time the situation gave the English a good excuse for military intervention. After they had allowed the indescribable slaughter to go on for a whole week, they began to fire their cannons upon the city from their ships, causing fires and much unnecessary destruction. Afterward, they imposed their rule upon the Egyptian people for seventy years.

Many Armenians, Maltese, and other foreigners, who lived in the poorer parts of the city, near the port, were killed. Sharia Saba Banat—Rue des Soeurs, as it was known to the Europeans—was nearly razed. But after that, things were quiet for decades.

Just after the Second World War, the Egyptians began to rebel once more. Nationalism was again on the rise. There were daily demonstrations in the streets. The slogan was 'al-Galaa'—out with the British bases, out with the British forces.

Then came the Arab–Israeli war, when the newly established state of Israel was attacked by its neighboring countries. For the Arabs the consequences of the confrontation were tragic. With corrupt leadership, poorly equipped, unprepared for war, the Arabs were routed.

Their wounded national pride, particularly that of the Egyptians, took its revenge where it could: on the Europeans, who watched the demonstrators smashing and looting their shops. The Egyptians were consumed by it. Out with the Zionists, out with the foreign spies. And the foreigners who had lived alongside them for more than three generations gradually began to leave.

•

The *Pobeda* made a great impression on me. It was a white ship, a modern passenger liner. The photographs I saw in the newspapers bore no resemblance to the gray warships that had crowded the port of Alexandria during the war.

This white vessel would carry off the Armenian family who lived opposite us, on the second floor of the gray *okella*. I had never actually seen them, but I had heard my mother saying over and over again, "They're all leaving. Even the Armenians across the way."

"What Armenians?" my aunt Magdalene asked—she was quite the gossip and she could not quite work out how she had missed this tidbit.

"The Armenian printer, you know, the one married to the seamstress . . . they've got two daughters. Quite how they'll leave, I don't know," added my mother. "The little one's very poorly."

I had never seen the little Armenian girl. I heard later that she was around nine or ten—about my age—a pretty, dark girl with huge black eyes. They said she was extremely bright, top of her class.

As the date of the ship's arrival approached, so the little girl's health worsened. The whole neighborhood was whispering about it, as if it were a secret that should not be divulged. They said she had leukemia.

"She won't live, poor thing," my mother said.

"What can they do? The ship'll be here next Sunday. How will they go? But how can they stay?"

Andriani, our neighbor from upstairs, who used to visit the Armenian family, said they had already emptied the house of their belongings. They had sold some things and sent others off to customs in trunks. Their tickets and passports were ready. But how could they leave with a dying child?

That sad story had shocked me. I would go to and from the window that overlooked the road and press my face against the window pane to try to see the *okella* across from ours. The shutters were always half-closed in the poor little girl's room. I would get up in the middle of the night, and at the crack of dawn; there was always a dim light glowing in the window opposite. The dark wings of death had never touched me before. Death was something that happened to the aged, like my Italian grandmother who had died because she was very old. For the first time I was becoming aware that death threatened little children too.

As soon as I got home from school, I would ask my mother, "How's the little girl across the way?"

"The same," she'd say, shaking her head sadly.

And so Monday, Tuesday, Wednesday, and Thursday passed. As Sunday approached, so did the white ship, and so did death.

•

In those days my brother and I used to go to the French school. My father wanted us to learn foreign languages. The French schools had a good reputation. It was a Catholic school, run by monks, so there were regular prayers, scripture classes, and church services. As I was Orthodox I could be excused from attending church services and, like my Muslim and Jewish classmates, was allowed to stay in the schoolyard while the others were at prayer. But I used to go to church because I enjoyed the hymns and psalms, the great organ, and the smell of incense. I would gaze at the statues of Christ in the arms of the Virgin, the waxen faces of the saints, sometimes sweet, sometimes austere. The priest would come and go, crossing himself, kneeling, rising again, blessing the congregation.

The service was held in Latin, so of course none of the children understood a word. The sermon, though, was in French. The priest was a good preacher, and always managed to leave us feeling guilty about our insignificant little sins.

I knew my teacher was pleased that I went to church, and he tried to convert me to Catholicism. Me, I just wanted to be on good terms with my teachers, and the fact that I attended the Catholic Church of Sainte Catherine with the school and the Orthodox Church of the Annunciation of the Virgin with my grandmother did not concern me at all. But whichever church I was in, I took care to cross myself in the Orthodox fashion, with the first three fingers held tightly together, starting with the forehead and touching first right and then left. That was the only difference as far as I could understand—that the Catholics crossed themselves with the hand open, touching first the left shoulder and then the right.

One day, the monk who taught us scripture confused me by telling me I was a heretic. Not that I was worried that I might be burned at the stake. I knew that this did not happen any more. That job had been taken over by the devils in Hell. There was a painting in our church depicting a terrible scene with ugly creatures, like winged goblins with little purple eyes, skewering the poor sinners. I trembled at the sight of that scene and always took care to sit where I could not see it. So I was surprised by the word 'heretic' and wondered what awful thing I had done to deserve it. Even though the good monk had smiled kindly as he said this harsh word, I did not feel good about it. He continued, stroking his snowy, patriarchal beard, "Arius was a heretic, which is a well-known fact." He said this with such disarming certainty that he almost convinced me, but then I thought, "Who is this Arius, anyway, and why should I be to blame for what he did, or failed to do?"

I remained uneasily quiet. At which point the monk was inspired to say, "One day, the Grace of the Lord may touch you—who knows? Don't you want to go to Paradise?"

I did not say anything, but I have to admit that I was not overly impressed by the idea of going to Paradise. I had seen some lithographs showing angels and saints. They presented an image of boring serenity. They certainly had a better time there than in Hell, but not as good as I had playing with my friends in the little neighborhood park.

•

As I thought about the little Armenian girl who was rushing toward death, I remembered all the hopeful, comforting things that I had read or heard about miracles, about Lazarus and the miracle-working saints whose names fill the church calendar. I remembered the sermons I had heard about faith and the power of prayer. I prayed with all the faith a child's soul can muster. If, as they said, faith could move mountains, then surely mine would block the road to death.

Yet between Thursday night and Friday morning the little girl died. They buried her in something of a hurry the next day, and the day after that the whole family left, along with the other passengers on the white ship. Perplexed by this sudden clash with reality, I tried to understand what had happened. The adults around me seemed to be familiar with the games fate plays. They knew. They knew that at times like these God and the saints do not interfere.

"God has taken her to Him, poor thing," someone said. "It's better this way. She's at peace now."

And fat Magdalene said, "Unfortunate soul, she didn't last long enough to see the land of her forefathers. It was her fate to stay here. So it was written."

But why, I wondered. Why was it so written? Who is making the decisions? Who is the writer of the fate of humans? Who has the right to share out pain? Why did they all lie to me?

•

The white ship left for the north with her Armenian passengers, all looking forward with hungry eyes toward the new land. All, that is, except for a mother, a father, a sister, who stood on the stern of the ship and watched the Great City fade away into the distance. One by one, the houses disappeared, as did the faces of people known and loved. Then the churches with their high bell towers and the mosques with their slender minarets faded away. With a turn of the wheel Qaitbey, the fort of the Eastern Harbor, vanished.

For a while, a hazy distant line remained on the horizon, and then that too was gone. Nothing was left but the immensity of the sea, the mute, unbearable pain, and when the tears had dried, impotent despair.

The Maestro

They used to call him Maestro. As children, we were not particularly interested in knowing what his real name was. He played the guitar, the bouzouki, the mandolin, and the banjo. He gave music lessons to the children of acquaintances' families in order to scrape together a meager living—to put a little food on his table and some pin-money in his pocket. As if it were not enough that the Maestro was poor and world-weary, he was also blind. Or perhaps I should say that he could barely see, because I often noticed him turn toward the light and hold some object up close, as if he were trying to make out its indistinct outlines.

Was the old Maestro a good musician? Who knows. He may have been. He definitely knew his music and played with passion. I liked to listen when he was giving lessons to my friend Michalis, who lived opposite us, two doors down, and I enjoyed his playing old songs on his guitar, *barcaroles* and *accompagnamenta*.

They said he had lost his sight in the war. In which war, I wondered? My knowledge of history being almost nonexistent, I thought to ask someone older and wiser than myself, but whenever I did so, I soon regretted it and was left with my eager thirst for knowledge unquenched.

Whenever I asked my elders some question or other—just simple everyday things—their usual reply was that I would understand when I grew up, and so I soon realized that they could not really be bothered to deal with my childish curiosity. On occasions when I actually did get an answer, rather than solving my problem it would simply add to my questions and confuse me even more.

I remember the day I saw a dead bat for the very first time. Curious, I asked my mother what it was. I thought this creature which looked like a mouse but flew like a bird was extraordinary. In response, my mother scared me half to death by telling me that if a bat were to catch its grasping little claws in my hair, I would never ever be able to get it off me. As thousands of bats could be seen flying around every evening, I lived for quite some time with the ghoulish vision of spending the rest of my life with a bat stuck to my head.

Another time, I asked my grandmother something, I do not remember quite what it was, but she replied, "What do you want to know that for? What's it to you? Goodness, that was years ago, child, way back in the time of the Genoese."

Of course, I was none the wiser for her remark, but those 'Genoese' started to really worry me. I asked my grandmother over and over again, but I do not think she really knew who the 'Genoese' were either. She had simply heard this expression used in Chios when she was a child, whenever anyone was talking about things that had happened long ago.

Were they human? Were they of this world or the other? The harsh expression with which my grandmother covered her own ignorance caused me to place the cursed 'Genoese' beyond the dark borders of myth, together with the bogeyman and the other fantastic fairy-folk who frightened me daily into finishing off my food, or worse still, swallowing that awful spoonful of cod-liver oil.

"Drink it up," I was told, "or the bogeyman'll get you."

"But why?" I would sob.

Because I was, apparently, too thin and if I did not take my medicine like a good boy, I would not grow. Haunted by the dreadful prospect of the bogeyman and the alarming example of Uncle Gaetano—who was short and humpbacked because, they said, he had not taken his cod-liver oil as a child—I would take a deep breath, pinch my nose and gulp down the disgusting potion, letting out as I did so such a terrifying wail that the other children thought that I really had been grabbed by the bogeyman.

•

But let us get back to the Maestro and the war. For us children the war was something abstract. Even though we were brought up during the Second World War with daily blackouts and air raids, we could not distinguish between the real war, where men took leave of their senses and turned into wild beasts, and the war games which we played. War for us was the two camps we divided ourselves into, each with officers and men. The loudest, the strongest, the eldest got to be officers. They never even asked the others, the weaklings, the shy, quiet ones, what they wanted to be—they were just automatically assigned to be ordinary foot-soldiers. In our wars, our battles, the officers were never killed. Only the soldiers fell, and even they soon got up again. That is what I thought real war to be like too, except that real soldiers had real guns that spewed out death. Our weapons were made from broomsticks, sugar cane, pared-down palm stalks. We would take aim and fire, shouting "Bam, bam, you're dead!" Death, pain, sorrow, all became just a joyful game. Fortunately, children are so far from knowledge and wisdom that they become immortal.

In which war had the Maestro lost his sight? It could not have been the last one, which had just ended. He was too old to have been in that war, anyway. He could have fought in the war of 1920, or in the previous Great War, or even in 1912. He was of that unfortunate generation that had not been able to discard their army boots and greatcoats in over ten years.

And how did he come to be in Alexandria? How and when had this stricken ship foundered in the Eunostos port? When you are young, you do not even ask; you do not take the time to think about such details. You pass them by in your eagerness to move on, to get ahead. But now that the years have passed, now that I am no longer young, I pause and bring all those images back to mind, all those people who had so very much to tell and who, in my haste, I neglected, paying no attention to their presence. An endless parade of soundless forms that often keeps me company at night. It is not a procession of ghosts, not faded figures enriched by fantasy. No, it is a complete tableau, rendered with sure, strong brushstrokes, three-dimensional and very much alive. All the people in this picture are moving, even those—and indeed, it is most of them—who are no longer of this world. In a corner, not among the protagonists, aside, is the Maestro, unaltered by time, just the same as he ever was, just as I remember him at Michalis' house.

The guitar lesson begins. With gentle, sure movements, the Maestro takes his guitar out of its case. How proud he was of that guitar. It was Spanish, he said. He touches it tenderly, caresses it, rests it against his chest and lowers his head. With empty eyes he gazes down at it and, sightless as he is, sees it in his heart, just as one feels a beloved one.

Thin, even weedy, the Maestro had strong arms and calloused fingers that could not always have caressed the cords of a guitar, which must for many years have been accustomed to harder work. Of medium height and upright bearing, he always held his head erect when he walked. His face was shriveled and rugged, marked by time and pain, with abnormally deep lines, like those often depicted on the faces of Byzantine saints. Many years before, his eyes must have been light blue, but now all color had been washed away; they were lifeless and sunken deep into their sockets below the arches of his heavy brows. His hair was thick, curly and as white as cotton wool, unruly and always badly combed. His face was completed by a thin nose, as straight as if it had been drawn with a ruler, and underneath it a small, neat mouth, with inconspicuous lips. He had a deep dimple in his chin that stood out almost like a scar and which was only just distinguishable from the wrinkles on his tired, old face.

I remember he was rarely clean-shaven. It seems he had trouble shaving and only occasionally made the effort, on Sundays and holidays. On those occasions he would arrive with his cheeks cut to shreds, as if he had been in a fight with cats.

And yet, the face of the Maestro was beautiful. It had taken on that appearance that the passage of time gives to ancient stones. What is there to admire in a newly erected column? It holds no memories, it has nothing to tell. The same is true of the well-preserved, rosy face, gently scented with lavender. But the fallen column, toppled by time, rutted by winds and rain, cries out, "I was here when Caesar wounded the Bruicheion. I was here on that terrible night when barbarians, cross in hand, murdered Hypatia. I was here when they destroyed the Soma of Alexander, that most magnificent monument."

The fallen column, the stones of a tumbled tower, these are monuments, just like the old Maestro himself. They carry with them the memory of our tribe. These are our monuments that mark the lengthy path of our own history.

●

The Maestro was a good man, a man of few words, polite; and, as often is the case with humble folk, he had dignity and pride. He dressed like a poor man, in old, used clothes that had been handed down to him by friends. They never quite fit him and were always either a little too large or too small. He never wore a tie, at a time when all Europeans in Alexandria, even those less well-off, wore neckties. He wore his shirt buttoned up to the neck, right to the last button.

They said that he came from Tsirigo. Where was Tsirigo? Some island of the Greek Archipelago.

The Maestro was alone in the world, all alone. He had neither a wife nor any family or relatives. He lived in the abandoned wash-house high on the flat roof of an old building in the Attarin district. No one ever entered his tiny room other than Aisha, the widow of the janitor, a fat Egyptian woman who came in to clean for him from time to time.

Sometimes people would tease him about her. "So how's Aisha then, Maestro?"

"She's fine," he would reply curtly, putting an end to the conversation.

•

Late in the afternoon, when the lesson was over, Michalis' mother would make the old teacher a cup of coffee, which he would slowly sip with obvious pleasure. As he sipped, his cheeks formed deep grooves, like empty bellows, where his back teeth were missing. When he had finished off his coffee he would drink a little cold water and wait for Michalis' mother to come and take away the tray.

"Many thanks, Kyria Fotini," he would say quietly, almost in a whisper.

Then she would leave him alone. The children played in the back room or went outside to play in the street. Kyria Fotini would be in the kitchen preparing the evening meal, which was never served until her husband Grigoris, who worked as an accountant, got home.

There in the corner of the small salon, sitting on the velvet couch with his hands on his knees, the Maestro would remain, quite still, sometimes turning his face toward the last rays of sunlight, which crept through the slats of the heavy Venetian blinds. As the light slowly faded, he would pick up his guitar and, very softly, play some Spanish melody. He played so gently, almost caressing the strings. He played for his own pleasure, for himself alone, as if he had no desire for anyone else to hear.

As the evening drew in and the last of the light faded, Kyria Fotini would put on the lights in the dining room and begin setting the table for dinner. The cheerful, homely sound of the dishes being laid out and the clatter of cutlery could be heard, while from the kitchen there came the appetizing aroma of the evening meal simmering gently on the Primus stove. The Maestro would allow a few more minutes to pass, and then he would stand, pick up his thick walking stick, which he always left in the same place, and make to leave.

"It's late. I'll be on my way," he would announce when he heard Kyria Fotini's portly form pass close by. "I'll leave you to your meal."

"Sit you down, Maestro," the good-hearted housewife would reply. "Where are you off to now? Grigoris will be here in a minute. You must stay and eat with us."

The Maestro would pause, as if giving the invitation some consideration, then he would return his stick to its place and sit down again.

•

And so the days passed, the years passed. Michalis gave up his guitar lessons, and his younger brother took up the mandolin.

The Second World War came to an end. The soldiers who had crowded the streets of the Great City departed. The Scots with their strange kilts, the Australians and New Zealanders with their wide-brimmed khaki hats, the Indians with their beautifully arranged beards and imposing turbans. Our own sailor boys with their close-cropped little mustaches and raffish swagger, the Poles with their heavy boots, which stank of sweaty feet. They all went home. The lucky ones, that is. The others remained forever in the desert. Immense are the graveyards of El Alamein. So many young lives were lost! Some are buried under a stone slab, a cross bearing their name and the title of the corps they had served in. Others remain anonymous, buried in mass graves. To the left of the road that cuts through the desert is the Allied cemetery; further on to the right, toward the sea, is the German. A little further still, the Italian. The enemies of yesteryear lie side by side now that the thunder of the cannons has died down.

But not all the surviving soldiers left. The English maintained their bases on the Suez Canal and a number of their boys stayed in Alexandria. The Egyptians, however, wanted independence, and angry demonstrations soon began. "Out, English, out!" the demonstrators would chant. "Foreign troops out!" and they would pelt the shops of Europeans with stones.

The English had been using a building behind our house as an army store for years, and the windows at the back of our apartment had been boarded up so as not to look out onto it. These neighboring stores were some of the easier targets for the demonstrators. They were close to the Arabic quarter dominated by the imposing granite column of Diocletian, known as Pompey's Pillar.

The scene was always the same: a couple of hundred locals would gather—the younger ones to the fore, the elder ones bringing up the rear. They would advance in tight formation, taking up the whole width of the street, chanting slogans as they went. When they reached the small mosque of Salah al-Din, right next to our building, they would find the road blocked by Egyptian policemen, the *shawish*, as we called them. Dressed in black throughout the winter and white in the summer, the *shawish* wore ridiculously wide trousers and great clumsy boots. When they had to deal with a demonstration like this, they would leave their red fezzes back at the station and don army helmets instead. As for weaponry, in their left hands they carried light wooden shields to protect themselves from stones, and in the right, long wooden sticks.

The confrontation would generally take place with little obvious enthusiasm on either side. Poorly paid, the policemen performed their duty without great zeal, their main concern being to return safely home at the end of the day. They would crouch down behind their shields and stoically take the barrage of stones hurled by the crowd. When this pelting was over, the police would move toward the demonstrators, holding up their sticks intimidatingly. The crowd would retreat. Anyone who fell during this exchange was trodden underfoot and received a thrashing from the sticks of the *shawish*. But the retreat only lasted as long as it took for the demonstrators to gather a fresh supply of 'missiles' and to regroup. Then the whole scene would be replayed—stones were thrown, the policemen would retreat, back and forth, back and forth. From time to time there would be injuries, blood would be spilled, bones would be broken.

When the demonstrators reached the barred gates of the English army stores, the second stage of the action would begin: English soldiers would appear behind the retreating Egyptian policemen. Redheaded, weary from the long war they had just won, they stood with their weapons at their sides. On seeing them, the crowd would hesitate; some of the youngsters in the front line would even run off. The crowd would pull back but continue to chant its slogans. The English troops would form two lines and ostentatiously load their weapons with a loud rattle of metal on metal. The rear line stood while the front line knelt and took aim. A hail of stones came from the crowd. In response, the soldiers discharged their rifles, aiming above the heads of the demonstrators. And that was that. The troops, with the undeniable superiority of strength which their firearms gave them, advanced upon the dispersing crowd at a steady pace for a hundred meters or so. The demonstrators scattered.

These events frightened the Europeans, who felt that their time in the Great City was coming to an end. And indeed the end had also come for the Greeks, the largest and best organized of the foreign communities.

The Maestro realized the situation and was worried by all this. Most of his pupils had already left the country. Michalis' family was making preparations to leave. Their eldest son, Costas, who had just gotten married, was heading for South Africa. Michalis, with his younger brother and parents, would be going to Greece. Their uncle Alekos and his children were planning to move to Australia. My family was making arrangements to leave for Brazil.

One evening, as they were getting up from the table, Grigoris decided it was time. He had already discussed this with his wife, Fotini. They would have to tell him the truth. They would have to reveal their plans to the Maestro. But there was no easy way to go about it. Grigoris took him aside, and they sat down together in the salon with the velvet chairs. He offered him a cigarette and started to talk about his work. The Maestro listened attentively.

"Things are not going well, Maestro," said Grigoris.

He cleared his throat, swallowed hard, lit a cigarette himself—something he rarely did in the house. He went on. "Fewer and fewer ships are coming into port these days. I mean," he explained, "the English ships we represent." He took a deep breath.

"The boss has brought in an Egyptian partner. Now we'll have to keep the books in Arabic . . . I don't know how to write Arabic." He said this very quietly, almost to himself. In fact, although the Greeks of Egypt all spoke Arabic, very few actually knew how to write it.

"They're letting me go," he whispered.

Grigoris got up from his armchair and paced around nervously. Then he stopped in front of the Maestro.

There was a long silence.

"We're talking of leaving, going to Athens. Things have quieted down there now."

It was done; he had said it, and, feeling that a great weight had been lifted from his chest, he sat down again. The Maestro did not say a word. He had lowered his head as if in thought. Suddenly he broke the silence, asking, "All being well, when will you be off?"

"In two or three weeks; somewhere around mid-August, the feast of the Virgin Mary," Grigoris replied.

"Ah, I see," said the Maestro.

He clasped his hands, unclasped them, rubbed his palms together uneasily, lowered his head once again. Then he turned his face toward Grigoris, and it was as if by sheer willpower he had regained his sight, if only for a brief moment; his empty gaze seemed to focus and his eyes took on the expression they normally lacked. He spoke, not with his voice, but with these piteous eyes that seemed to be asking: and what will become of me? Where does all this leave me?

But that spark was soon gone and his gaze was once again blank and empty. He made an attempt to speak, but though his lips moved, no sound came from his dry throat. Silence once more.

All was still. Kyria Fotini stood perplexed in the doorway. Only the pendulum of the old German wall clock seemed unmoved by the drama being played out before it and continued its monotonous ticking. The couch creaked as the Maestro stood up. He looked large, imposing, as if he had suddenly grown in stature. As if this pain had given him supernatural size.

He took up his walking stick and, as always, in a low, gentle voice he said, "Many thanks, Kyria Fotini."

He groped his way out of the small sitting room and walked down the long, darkened hallway that led to the front door.

Grigoris rushed ahead of him and pulled back the bolt, then removed the heavy safety bar, while Fotini turned the key three times in the lock and opened the door.

"Goodbye, Maestro. We'll talk again soon," said Grigoris. But it was only with great difficulty that the Maestro managed a throttled "Goodnight."

The couple listened as the old man went down the stairs, tapping out each step with the point of his stick. When all was silent in the stairwell, they closed the door again. The key could be heard turning three times, the bolt being drawn, then the thump of the safety bar being secured. Kyria Fotini looked up at her husband with tears in her eyes, but said nothing. Grigoris avoided her gaze and said, "What can we do? What else can we possibly do?"

•

It was a Saturday evening, I remember. It was summer. We always looked forward to Saturday evenings, as they brought with them the promise of Sundays; but Saturday evenings during the summer were especially sweet. Although the day was hot, the sunset brought with it a soothing breeze. We youngsters would dress up and go to the Greek Athletic Club in Chatby. There, friends who had sometimes not seen each other all week would gather and sit around outside at the tables set out in the garden above the sports ground. The gentle breeze blowing in from the sea brought with it the scent of moonflowers and jasmine. We would listen to music, Greek music, drink lemonade and talk about the sporting events that were to be held the following day, about the film we would see at the cinema on Sunday evening, and, in furtive whispers, about the girls.

The girls who came to the club would always sit separately from the boys, in small groups or with their parents. Occasionally, they would sneak a glance or a smile in our direction and then burst into stifled giggles, while we would strain out of the corners of our eyes to see who it was that Stella was looking at, or who Rena had smiled at.

There was Stella, with her boyishly short-cropped, jet-black hair, sitting with Rena, her younger sister, who was always following in her shadow. And Maria, whose huge blue eyes, it seemed, held the very sky itself. Myrto, who was always so serious, and quite an athlete, sat chewing gum. Then there was Renio, the short one with the stubby legs and blonde plaits. And the teacher's daughter, Fotini, who was full of freckles. So many trouble-free, easy-going boys and girls, who in a few short months would be separated forever. They would be scattered like dry leaves in the autumn breeze. But that evening there was no room for melancholy thoughts in our young heads. All you could hear were happy voices, laughter, and playful teasing; like a flock of fluttering, carefree sparrows.

•

As soon as he had left the building, the Maestro found himself all alone on the street. He set out to walk home, but after just a few steps he stopped and turned back. He walked toward the Attarin Mosque—an old mosque that stood proudly on the site of the old Church of Saint Athanasios, protector of the old town, now long lost. He turned right and with uncertain steps headed toward Rue Fouad. When he reached the Amir Cinema, he turned left and continued in the direction of Ramleh Station and the Corniche.

Only very rarely had the Maestro wandered so far from home. He generally kept to the familiar nearby streets, but on that evening he could not stand the idea of being restricted to his humble room, or confined to that same old neighborhood. It seemed that there was not room enough for him even in the whole of the Great City. As he walked, he mingled with the Saturday-night crowds strolling idly through the streets. Several times he bumped into people who had stopped to gape at the photographs displayed outside the cinemas. He passed outside the brasseries with their delicious *mezze*, the pastry shops that oozed the tempting aroma of chocolate, mille-feuilles, and crisp meringue.

At one point he was almost run down by a passing carriage. He was bewildered by the jangling of bells as the startled cabby swerved to avoid him, and the skidding of the horse's hooves as he was brought up short by the sudden jerk of the reins. Someone grabbed him by the arm and helped him across the road. It was there that Artin, the Armenian cobbler, out for a stroll with his wife, saw the Maestro. He says he spoke to him, but either the Maestro did not hear, or he pretended not to hear, and continued on his way.

Edgizio, the Italian typographer, who had studied the mandolin with the Maestro, saw him outside the Athenaios patisserie. He greeted him, but got no reply. The Maestro crossed the road and continued toward the old harbor, following the wall of the Corniche, toward the fort of Qaitbey, which stood at the far western point of the ancient harbor, casting its great, gray shadow just as the wondrous, ancient Pharos of the Ptolemies had done so long ago.

He continued to walk aimlessly, with no idea where he was headed. When he came to the statue of Ismail that stood looking out to sea, he suddenly felt very weary, as if his legs could no longer support him. How long had he been wandering about like this? An hour or two? Maybe more. Two little local kids playing catch careered into him and almost knocked him over. Befuddled, he sat down on the stone wall next to the granite steps of the monument, where he remained, motionless, for some time. He tried to catch his breath, to think things through, to put his thought into some sort of order, but it was impossible. Things were all jumbled up in his mind. He thought that if he could just bring back the memories of the good old days, those wonderful images of the past, then perhaps they would calm him down. But somehow they seemed to slip away from him, only to be replaced by memories of the hard times, memories that crowded in on him, forming a dark labyrinth from which there was no escape.

What would become of him when his last few pupils had left? He was not so much concerned by how he would earn a living as he was horrified by the yawning loneliness that opened up before him, exposing a darkness so much denser and more terrifying than the darkness he was used to, a darkness that stalked like a wild beast waiting to swallow him up. Every lesson was, for him, a visit to a friendly home, a warm chat with the lady of the house, a nice cup of coffee. These houses were his home, his family, his friends.

It was getting late. The babble of passers-by died down

and the streets fell quiet. Occasionally someone would rush past, in a hurry to get home. Even so, the night was sweet and strangely beautiful, inappropriately so. The Maestro strained his ears for the sound of any living soul, but all he could hear was the far-off sound of the sea as it tirelessly continued its centuries-old struggle with the ancient stones.

Suddenly he was struck by an almost primal fear—fear of the vast expanse of that deserted square. Thinking that perhaps he was dreaming, he shook himself, stood up, tried to get his bearings. He felt he was sinking into a nightmarish chasm, an empty nothingness beyond his control. In total panic he felt a desperate need to talk to someone, to touch a human hand. His heart began to pound, he was drenched in sweat, his whole body trembled and his teeth chattered loudly. He just stood there, unable to move, and when he tried to call for help, what escaped from his chest was not a human voice but a screech, a roar of pain, the howl of a wounded animal.

A lone passer-by rushed to see what was wrong, and called a couple of snoozing policemen to come and help. They found the Maestro unconscious, lying beneath the statue of the khedive. Taking him for a drunk, they dragged him to a nearby bench to sleep it off. He had taken a nasty bang as he fell, so at daybreak they took him to the Greek hospital, where the doctors managed to bring him round.

•

By Monday the news had spread and the Maestro's few remaining friends in Alexandria went to visit him.

"I knew it," sniffled Kyria Fotini as she related the story to Signora Angelina, the Italian lady from downstairs. "He was so upset when he left, I knew he'd have a nasty turn. He had trouble with his blood pressure, you know."

Thodoros, Kyria Sarantias' husband, suggested that they get the barber to apply leeches to suck out the bad blood.

"Leeches?" cried Angelina, who was a well-educated

young woman. "He's in the hospital, for goodness' sake. The doctors there have much more modern methods."

The doctors did what they could to save the Maestro, who, they said, had suffered a stroke. We went to visit him, but he seemed to have aged so much that he was almost unrecognizable. We tried to talk to him, but what could we say? The usual banalities that one says to the desperately ill:

"Chin up, Maestro, you'll be just fine. You'll be back home in no time."

"You get yourself well, and we'll all go for ice cream at Pastroudis'."

The Maestro seemed to be at ease; perhaps he was too tired to continue the struggle. The wounded beast was calm. When visitors talked too much, he became tired. He would flutter his hand dismissively as if saying, "Leave me in peace; leave me to die."

And so God, or whatever there is up there, took pity upon the old Maestro and took him without unnecessary suffering. During the few days he spent in the hospital, he never uttered a word. Could he not speak, or did he just have no desire to do so? Perhaps a little of both. But toward the end, Kyria Fotini, who was by his side day and night, heard him murmuring something indistinguishable as if in a strange, foreign chant—and a name: "Carmella."

He said it two or three times, almost as if he were singing.

"Must have been some old girlfriend of his," thought Kyria Fotini, with tears in her eyes.

Then the Maestro turned his face slightly toward the open window. The white tulle curtain battled vainly to keep out the harsh rays of the sun, but the insistent light poured in unashamedly anyway and lit up every inch of the white-walled sickroom.

"Farewell, comrades," said the Maestro. "It's time for me to go."

Frau Grete

"Come and see! Children, come and see! Look, it's snowing!"

Snow in Alexandria? Why, it seemed impossible, but Frau Grete was right; it really was snowing! She was absolutely ecstatic. She ran outside in her nightdress, out onto the small corner balcony which looked out over the sea, tearfully calling for the children to come outside and see the snow:

"Schnee! Schnee! . . . Komm Karl, komm Brigitte, Schnee! Schnee!"

The entire city was up and about. People were out on their balconies, down in the street. They stared unbelievingly at the lead-gray sky that seemed to be hanging so low you could almost touch it. They reached out to try to catch the wispy, white snowflakes as they fell to the ground, but in vain—as soon as you touched them they melted clear away.

If I remember right, it was 1947, or perhaps a year later. They said it had not snowed in Alexandria for a hundred years. For us children, it was a wonderful excuse to get out into the streets, to run about and make as much noise as possible.

I had only read about snow in story books like *Tom Thumb*, Charles Dickens' *A Christmas Carol*, and *Sans Famille* by Hector Malot. I would look at the snow-covered landscapes in books and yearn to see a real mountain for myself, a snow-capped peak, a forest of firs packed with squirrels, weasels, and foxes. These creatures hopped from the colored illustrations on the pages of my storybooks and kept me company in my childish dreams.

And now, it was actually snowing! Not that pretend stuff we decorated the Christmas tree with—but real snow!

For Frau Grete the event was exceptionally significant, especially moving. You will not think her tears extreme, or her reaction exaggerated, when I tell you that Grete was born in Germany, and had not seen snow since the day she arrived in Alexandria as a very young girl—over thirty years before.

When she had recovered from the initial shock, the first emotional reaction, Frau Grete felt obliged to make sure that this was not real snow falling. The flakes were fine and sparse, dissolving almost before they touched the ground. Nothing like the thick snow that fell in Konstanz, where she was born.

"Now *that* was snow!" Frau Grete said with some pride. The snow that fell in Alexandria but once in a hundred years was nothing in comparison, hardly worth calling snow at all, really.

"Ah, Karl, my sweet," she sighed, tenderly stroking her son's blond head, "will we *ever* go back home, I wonder?"

Silently, she gazed toward the distant horizon, as if trying to will herself across the sea to the distant Bodensee. She missed her homeland so very much: the cold, the snow, the fragrance of the forest. Thinking about it made her feel nostalgic, melancholy. She stood transfixed, almost in ecstasy. Below the little balcony, the sea had become strangely still, as if it had given up its age-old battle with the great rock that, in the muffled silence, loomed across the bay like a big, bald, mythical giant.

But it soon stopped snowing. Frau Grete went back inside. Disappointed, the children returned to their homework, and the sea slowly resumed its timeless, relentless rhythm.

•

Frau Grete was a beautiful, buxom Valkyrie of a woman, with quite an imposing manner. She had chestnut hair and white skin, with cheeks like wax that blushed at the slightest emotion. She had large, honey-colored eyes. She used to blacken her eyelashes impressively and emphasize the arch of her brows with two dark pencil lines. Her nose was quite straight, her mouth small, thin, and tight, with a slight dimple at the sides. But it was her hair that impressed me. I once saw her with her hair down—it fell in wonderful thick waves down her back, right to her waist. But in general, she wore it carefully tied up, a labyrinth of countless tightly-wound plaits forming a magnificent bun. It suited her; it emphasized her somewhat austere air.

I suppose she must have been around forty then. Maybe a little older; or perhaps the way she dressed made her seem more mature. Children can never judge the age of adults well.

When at home, she used to wear dark, ample dresses that she called 'peignoirs.' But whenever she went out, even when she went shopping, she would always go to great lengths with her appearance. She dressed well, with care, usually in a suit—a well-cut jacket and skirt. She often wore a hat to set off her outfit. Frau Grete's hats were a source of great amusement to me. They were brimming with feathers and flowers. One in particular was more unusual than most; it looked rather like a nest, right in the middle of which, packed in among all the feathers and down, you could just make out the tiniest little blue bird.

•

Grete had arrived in Alexandria with her parents just after the First World War. Her father, Karl Schröder, had been advised by doctors that the climate there would be good for his health. Together with a Jew and a Greek, he opened a shop selling off-the-rack menswear in the great Muhammad Ali Square, which was known at the time as 'Place des Consuls.' Herr Schröder was enterprising and his partners hard-working, and after just two years, they opened another shop in Saad Zaghloul Boulevard.

In those days, all the Europeans in Alexandria had their

suits handmade by tailors. Even shirts were made to order by specialist shirtmakers. So the few shops selling ready-to-wear garments, being a novelty, were making a fortune.

Schröder traveled frequently to all the major European capitals, especially to Berlin, Vienna, and Budapest, not only to order material and linings but also to keep up with what was being worn in Europe, to copy patterns and fashions.

One day Brigitte showed me her grandfather's passport. On the inside page was the yellowed photograph of a handsome man with great mustaches reaching right to his bushy sideburns. It was the same photograph that I had seen, enlarged and displayed in a heavily varnished frame, hanging on their living room wall. The following pages were covered with strange stamps—some circular in black ink, others triangular in blue ink, others square. We stumbled over the strange names of foreign ports, some written in letters we could make out, but others in unknown script. How hungrily we fingered those pages, just as we did the *laissez-passer* of my own grandfather, who was from mainland Greece and was also well-traveled. When would we ever get a chance to see the world? When would we escape the insidious sand dunes that surrounded the city? When would we set sail for unknown seas?

•

The few Germans who lived in Alexandria, like most other European inhabitants of the city, led a comfortable life in those peaceful years between the wars. The German community was small but well organized. The Germans were technicians, merchants, importers, and employees in shipping companies, insurance agencies, and other enterprises.

Grete, Herr Schröder's only daughter, grew into an attractive young woman. When she graduated from the high school run by German nuns, her father did not have a hard time finding a suitable husband for her. Olaf was a quiet, good-hearted German lad, born in Alexandria, whose parents had immigrated from Berlin. He was tall and handsome and wore his blond hair with a sharp part down the middle. He worked for a company that imported machinery for textile factories.

It was an arranged marriage, which was not unusual in those days. A year after the wedding, a son was born—the spitting image of his father. Grete decided to name him after her own father—Karl. A couple of years later, she gave birth to a pretty little girl, who was given the name of Olaf's mother, Brigitte. Brigitte was just like her mother, except that her hair was quite blond.

But those carefree years, when cosmopolitan Alexandria and the whole of Europe enjoyed such calm, were coming to an end. The dark clouds of fascism and Nazism were gathering on the horizon. In Madrid, the Spanish democrats died crying "No pasarán." But fascism won through. The democracies of Europe were weak, their townsfolk comfortable in their easy lives; they were unable to withstand such force, and, one after the other, fell victim to the lusty appetites of the dictators. And then war was declared.

Egypt, with her semi-colonial regime and bordering on Italian-held Libya, soon found herself embroiled in the action. Troops began to swarm in from all over the British Empire, and the port of Alexandria was soon packed with warships of all shapes and sizes. Then came blackouts, sirens, and the first air raids.

It was then that the British rounded up all the adult male Italians and Germans who lived in Egypt and interned them. There were thousands of Italians in the *camps d'internement*, but only a few Germans. Olaf was one of the first to be taken.

The Italian women howled inconsolably when their men were taken away, but Frau Grete took it all with calm composure. She never once complained all the time Olaf was in the internment camp; she never even referred to it, as if nothing untoward had actually happened. She would visit her husband whenever it was allowed, but when anyone asked,

"How's Olaf?" she would simply reply, "He's fine," as if she were humiliated that her husband was a prisoner and not fighting with his fellow countrymen on the front for the glory of the Third Reich. When Olaf was taken into custody, Grete's parents came to live with her and the children. The British were not concerned with Herr Schröder, who was elderly and in poor health.

•

Grete had always dreamed of traveling to Germany—not to stay permanently, she loved Alexandria—but she felt a nostalgic need to see the country of her birth once more.

"We'll go next year," she used to say, but there was always some reason why the trip was postponed at the last minute. Now she felt cut off from her homeland, trapped, helpless in an enemy country.

At the onset of hostilities, Grete followed the news of German victories with obvious pride. Despite the fact that we could receive only local radio stations—the others were masked by static interference—news of these events could not be kept from us. After a few short months, the Germans had conquered most of Europe. Later the fighting moved to North Africa. In 1942, Rommel, who had become a legend, crossed the Libyan border and entered Egypt. His first objective was Alexandria, his ultimate goal being control of the Suez Canal, to cut the allies off from access to the Indies and gain control of the oil fields of the Middle East.

For Alexandria, the wait was agonizing. News from the front worsened and the bombardment of the city became heavier and more frequent. The troops left Alexandria; they all moved west in a last desperate attempt to hold off the Axis forces. Some one hundred kilometers from Alexandria, in a narrow stretch of desert between the sea and the depression of Qattara, an insignificant little Bedouin village called El Alamein would go down in history as the theater of the greatest battle in North Africa.

Feelings were mixed in the city. The Egyptians, bewildered as they were by events, tried to stay out of it all, to escape the bombing as best they could. Most were packed into impoverished neighborhoods, with no air-raid shelters, and they were unable to protect themselves. Some of them secretly hoped that Rommel would prevail and take the city, that the Germans would conquer Egypt and liberate them from the yoke of English rule.

The Europeans, depending upon their origin, were divided into supporters of the Allies and sympathizers of the Axis. Naturally, the families of the Italians and Germans hoped that their troops would win. Encouraged by Rommel's advance, the Italians had begun demonstrations, timidly at first, but soon with more confidence. With Italian flags at the ready and photographs of the king and the Duce, they waited expectantly for the time to come when they could hang them out on their balconies. "Arrivano i nostri," they chanted arrogantly as they prepared to welcome the bersaglieri, who, in the event, never arrived. And the flags remained folded away in their trunks.

But the war continued to rage. Whichever side you were on you could not help but feel the fear, the terrible ordeal of the bombardments. At one point the air raids were daily, as the port was a prime target. More and more often, we would spend whole nights in the air-raid shelter. As soon as darkness fell, the first siren would be heard, a strident, hair-raising howl. And then the blackout. We came to anticipate the air raids and made sure we had already eaten before the siren sounded. When it did, we would go down into the shelters, in no great rush, as we knew we had three, four, even five minutes from the initial sounding of the alarm until the first enemy aircraft would appear over the city.

There were only a few shelters; they were makeshift affairs that had to serve whole blocks of buildings. To get to ours, we had to cross the road and walk some fifty meters. With the first wail of the siren, the roads would fill up briefly with silent human shadows, some in pajamas, nightdresses, dressing gowns, with babies in their arms, others carefully dressed up. But all moved like ghosts in the dark. With fearful faces turned upward toward the black night sky, we would strain our eyes to see if the searchlights had picked up the enemy aircraft.

The searchlights, located on the outskirts of the city, systematically scoured the sky. It was a sight both splendid and terrifying. The rays flooded the heavens like the threads of some giant spider's web, entrapping the enemy planes like tiny insects. When a plane was 'caught' in the web, you could see it clearly, way up in the sky. Like a small, bright, shining cross, seeming to move so slowly, trying vainly to escape. Then the anti-aircraft guns would start up and the shells would explode all around the trapped plane, filling the air with billowing smoke, like dusty clouds that glowed strangely in the beams of the searchlights.

I never saw more than that, because at the first thunder of the cannons, my mother would grab me by the hand and drag me, sometimes running, sometimes tumbling, down the steps into the shelter. Then the long wait would begin. It seemed to last forever.

The walls of the shelter were packed with sandbags, piled one on top of the other. A miscellaneous hotchpotch of seats were scattered about—old wobbly chairs, benches, stools, the occasional camp bed for the children to sleep on when the bombardment went on all night. Cramped, poorly ventilated and damp, the shelter stank of mold, stale breath, sweat, and smelly feet. Women, old people and children all piled in—the young men were gone; most were at the front or in the Air Defense Corps; others—'the enemy'—were held in internment camps.

During a raid everyone was absolutely silent—even the children. We did not feel like playing games anyway. Tired and miserable as we were, we knew that if we made any fuss at all, the slightest noise, we would get a swift slap. The worst part of it all, though, was that you could not cry. You had to swallow your sobs, as silent tears rolled down your cheeks.

I knew the adults were afraid. They were more frightened than we were, I think. I could see it in their faces as, wide-eyed, they looked nervously around, irritably shushing anyone who made a sound. They held their breath and waited. Even though the shelter was underground, dug deep into the bowels of the earth, we could hear the roar of the cannons clearly. As they started off intermittently in the distance, someone, unable to contain himself, would whisper, "That's the Mex cannon."

"Sssssh!" all the others would hiss together. Later the gunfire became more intense and ever closer. An old woman would whisper, "It's the guns at Silsila."

Then, a while later, an ominous explosion, like the calling of the archangel of the Apocalypse. It was the great cannon at Kom al-Dikka. Even I was scared of that cannon. It reverberated so loudly that the very foundations of the shelter shook, and startled cockroaches shot out of their hiding places among the sandbags.

I was terrified of cockroaches. Hidden among those sandbags were huge, winged, chestnut-colored cockroaches, which seemed to take a special delight in crawling so close to me . . . and I could not even scream. It was unbearable torture. Once an extra-big one ran right up my foot, and I let out such a shriek that I caused total panic in the shelter.

The cannon of Kom al-Dikka not only awoke the cockroaches in the *abri*, as we called the shelter, but in all the people enclosed within those walls it awoke an intense religious devotion. You could hear whispered prayers, as if each individual was praying to his own personal God, his own Prophet, his own Saint: "Virgin Mary, help us," "Holy Mother and San Antonio work your wonders," "Allah, Allah the merciful, have pity on us." But there was not room enough in that shelter for God, the Prophet, the Saints . . . and the bombardment went on and on.

From time to time it would go quiet, and then we would hear a whistling sound, followed by a deafening blast. A bomb had exploded nearby. They said that if you heard the whistling sound, you knew you were safe; that those destined to die in the blast never got to hear it at all.

At other times, the planes would fly so low that we could hear the throb of the engines. Aram, who was a mechanic and knew about such things, used to say, "That's a Stuka," or "That's an Italian."

We used to get in such a panic when we suspected that it was Italian planes attacking. The Germans always searched carefully for their target: the port. But the Italians just dropped their bombs wherever they could, eager to get out of there as soon as possible, impatient to get away from the anti-aircraft fire, not much caring where the bombs fell!

All that was fifty years ago now—half a century, goodness, how time flies . . . I remember those nights in the underground shelter as if they were only yesterday. The thunder of the cannon, the wailing of the sirens. I can still see the people around me, fearful, weary, defenseless, silent; all sorts of people: Italians, Greeks, English, Maltese, Armenians, Copts, Egyptians both Copts and Muslims, Slavs, Germans, and Jews.

●

Grete and her children did not go into the *abri* on every alert. Usually they stayed at home with Grete's parents. Old Herr Schröder was almost paralyzed and it was a struggle to get him down into the shelter, so they only went when there was heavy bombing.

But one dreadful night, they did come to the shelter. Grete helped her father, who dragged one leg as he walked and leaned heavily on a stick. Her mother followed behind with the children. That night a terrible thing happened; a bomb fell right in the heart of the Greek district of Ibrahimiya. It shook the whole shelter. In the confusion everyone was screaming, praying, crossing themselves, crying.

Grete was sitting on a low bench next to her parents. Karl was sitting next to his grandfather. Brigitte, next to her grandmother, was curled up like a frightened kitten, sobbing. Grete was pale. She looked a mess. She seemed to have aged. I wonder what was going through her mind, how she felt knowing that it was German planes that were bombing us.

Nino the Yugoslav, whose Italian wife, Irma, was an artist, ran out into the street to see what was happening. Not out of courageousness, but out of curiosity. He was so terrified that he was suffocating in there, he just had to get out. He came straight back inside, in a terrible state, his eyes wide, his teeth chattering in shock.

He could not get a word out. They gave him some water to drink out of a pitcher, but his hands were shaking so much that he spilled most of it. He collapsed onto a nearby camp bed and stuttered, "They've all gone. All the houses have gone. We'll never get through the night alive!"

He was exaggerating somewhat. The houses were still standing. A few balconies had crashed to the ground, windows were broken. I do not think there was a pane of glass left intact in the whole neighborhood. Right at the beginning of the war, we had stuck strips of paper in the shape of the Union Jack on all the windows, not out of love for the British, but so that if the windows were to shatter, the sharp pieces would stick to the paper.

A bomb fell at the junction just down the road from the shelter. It left a great crater, gorged deep into the heart of the ancient earth, waking the sleep of quite a few of our ancestors in the process. Again there was a commotion of sobbing, weeping and prayers, all mixed up in the noisy barrage of anti-aircraft fire, as the air-defense forces desperately struggled to repel the metal war-hawks as they spat out death and destruction.

"Damned Germans," yelled old Matina. "They'll slaughter us all tonight. Butchers! Murderers!"

The captive residents of the shelter could take no more.

They all felt they had to *do* something: shout, cry, curse the enemy who, for months now, had deprived them of their husbands, their sons, their sleep, their peace of mind, their comfortable lives. They were on the brink of panic. As they swore at the German pilots, they looked toward Frau Grete—'the German.' They did not look her in the eye, but cast sideways glances at her, sometimes threateningly, sometimes contemptuously.

In the middle of the bombing, at the height of the pandemonium, Grete got up. She arranged her dark shawl around her shoulders and signaled to her father to stand, which he did, with some difficulty. He did not say a word, but looked across at his neighbor Ismail, the upholsterer, as if to say: Why am I to blame?

Then the old Berliner, with the help of his daughter, limped over to the stairs and began to climb them painfully. The children followed with their grandmother. Brigitte had stopped crying, but she kept sniffing annoyingly. When they reached the top of the stairs, Grete opened the iron door. It squeaked on its hinges. At once, the flashes from the cannon-fire burst into the shelter as if they had been waiting outside for just this moment. But Grete did not hesitate. She pulled the collar of her father's coat up—it was rather cold out—and they went outside. They walked slowly down the road, with shards of burning hot metal falling all around them—shrapnel from the shells fired by the anti-aircraft guns.

That night was followed by many other nights of bombardment, but Frau Grete and her family never came down to the shelter again.

We moved out of the city. My mother's uncle Gaetano put us up in his house in Sidi Bishr for a few months. That way, my father said, we would escape the bombing. And we did, too.

The war went on for another two years, but moved farther and farther away from North Africa, from Alexandria. The air raids became less frequent and finally ceased altogether.

We returned to the city. I remember the English had brought some huge German tanks back with them from the desert as trophies. They were displayed in one of the big squares, I do not remember which one. But I do remember my father taking me to see them. Fascinated, young and old alike explored the stricken beasts. We climbed up, stepping on the tracked wheels, and clambered inside, each looking for some small souvenir of the impotent dragon to take home with us. My memento was an empty machine-gun clip. I did not know exactly what it was, but I examined it with my friends, turning it this way and that, poking around, until I finally managed to get my finger stuck inside and cut myself on the spring.

A few years later I saw such armored vehicles, with their gray-green camouflaged bodywork, marked with black crosses, abandoned in the desert, left to rust and oblivion. From El Alamein to Marsa Matruh, Sollum and all the way to the outskirts of Tripoli, from Cyrenaica to Tobruk, the desert was scattered with tanks, jeeps, and various other machines of warfare. These, and countless minefields, marked out the narrow stretch of coastal land, silent witnesses to the savagery of war.

The battles continued on other fronts. Hitler's Germany and Mussolini's Italy, which had so lavishly sown the seeds of war, now reaped nothing but great piles of rubble, and the earth gorged itself on enough blood and tears to last for generations. From the smoking ruins, it was impossible to distinguish the conquerors from the conquered. And when they had all had enough of killing and being killed, the long-awaited day came, and peace was declared.

I remember how relieved my father was when he rushed home and told us the news. It was midday. He had just gotten in from work, and the minute he entered the house, breathlessly, before he had even handed the two loaves of bread he had brought home to my mother, he announced, "The war's over, at last, the torture's over."

I was in something of a quandary. I was not really sure whether I should celebrate noisily and jump for joy, or take the news solemnly. I hesitated. I remembered how, at the outbreak of war, my father had announced that he might be called up to active service—in the end he was not—and I had rushed to celebrate. I thought he would have liked to wear a uniform and carry a gun, a real rifle. Apparently not. I was given a right telling off. They said I was insensitive. But the war did not bother me much, often the reverse; I sometimes found it quite fun.

Now what are we going to do without the war? I wondered. We had gotten used to it.

•

Frau Grete was inconsolable. She could not believe that Germany had been defeated. It seemed inconceivable to her that they had lost the war. And she could not accept that the Führer was dead. She claimed it was all a lie, a shameless fabrication put about by English and Jewish propaganda. It was just not possible that the great Leader was gone. He must be in hiding somewhere, and one day he would surely show himself.

On the Fox Movietone newsreels that were shown every week at the cinema, we saw scenes of a defeated and destroyed Germany. Berlin was unrecognizable, Hamburg and Dresden were nothing but piles of rubble, whole towns and villages were razed, wiped off the map. We witnessed endless lines of German prisoners of war—unshaven, ragged, eyes sunken into their heads from fear, exhaustion, and hunger, dragging their heavy boots as they trudged down muddy roads.

It made you feel almost sorry for them, seeing the warriors of the once unbeatable Wehrmacht filing down the road, their wounds bandaged with torn rags, leaning on improvised crutches. But how could you feel sorry for them? How could you forgive? How could you forget, when these scenes were followed by blood-curdling pictures of the concentration camps: Dachau, Buchenwald, Auschwitz, Belsen? We struggled to pronounce those names that would later become synonymous with horror; we had trouble believing it all.

My parents, sitting on either side of me in the darkened cinema, would try to cover my eyes. My mother told me not to look. "Such things aren't for children to see."

And, pretending to do as I was told, I would cover my face with my hands, but I could not help peeking through my fingers to see those skeletal, naked bodies being dumped from vans into a huge, tumbling heap. And those who were alive moved across the screen slowly, soundlessly, in total futility, like Dante's damned. They stared vacantly into the camera lens intruding upon their plight, with the most enormous eyes, eyes far too big for their emaciated faces, empty eyes that held neither pain nor hatred nor shame. I was too young to be able to comprehend such cruel savagery, such infinite anguish. But the scenes were indelibly etched upon my mind, where they remained for future analysis.

Did Frau Grete see these newsreels? Yes, she did. She saw the downfall of the nation that she had so admired. But she refused to believe what she saw, blaming it all on Jewish propaganda. Perhaps in the beginning she honestly believed this was true. After all, it was simply not possible that this superior race of blond demigods, who had envisioned a better world, a fine world, a well-disciplined society—it was not possible that they could do such things.

"Don't forget," I heard her say once, "that the Jews used to make their bread with the blood of Christian children."

And she had unshakeable evidence to support this. All the 'crimes' of the Jews were recorded in a book that she had at home. That really made me think. To me, whatever was printed in black and white automatically had to be the absolute truth.

•

There were many Jews in Alexandria. They were all over the place, in every part of the city and in every walk of life. There were very rich Jews and very poor Jews. Some of them must have been descendants of the Jewish community of the city in Ptolemaic times. They all spoke Arabic and there was nothing in their appearance to differentiate them from the other Egyptians. Others came later from North Africa, and from the Iberian Peninsula. They came to the welcoming city of Alexandria, victims of the Spanish Inquisition, and they spoke their own dialect mixed with Spanish. Others came from Central Europe, speaking Yiddish, a language with German roots. But the variety did not stop there—there were Jews from the Levant, Greek Jews, French Jews, Italian Jews, and every other possible mixture you could imagine.

I cannot claim that the Jews were particularly popular with the Christians. After all, as Frau Grete said, "Weren't Jews responsible for the crucifixion of Christ?"

My grandmother once told me that in Chios, during the celebration of the Resurrection, they used to burn the image of 'the Hebrew.' But I could not help wondering: If it weren't for the Jews, how would Christ have been crucified? And if he hadn't been crucified, how would we have been saved? Obviously, I could not begin to answer such theological questions. I had all sorts of doubts and countless queries, but I put them aside, preferring instead to play with sweet Brigitte, who cared little for all that.

Soon Olaf returned, looking plump and healthy, as if he had been on holiday. Life slowly resumed its old rhythm, just like it was before the war. But not for long. After the Palestinian war that followed the proclamation of the state of Israel, all the Jews left. The Egyptian enmity toward them was so intense that they gathered up their belongings and departed. Some went to the land of their forefathers, the 'Promised Land,' others to France or Italy, if they had relatives there. Many emigrated to America and Canada. When the Jews had gone, and after the short war that followed the nationalization of the Suez Canal, the English, French, and Italians left. Later the Greeks.

So Alexandria, a cosmopolitan city since its very foundation, suddenly found herself inhabited only by Egyptians. The city to which the poet had prophetically bid farewell fifty years before was vanishing forever. One after the other, we all bid our own farewells.

•

Things were difficult for Olaf and his family. The company he worked for had closed, and the family had no relatives in Germany. Germany, defeated and divided down the middle, was licking the wounds of her body and soul. The children were growing up. Where could they go? Gradually Grete came to realize that they could not go back to Germany and they began to make preparations to emigrate to Brazil, which in those days encouraged European immigrants.

"There are lots of Germans there," Olaf assured his wife. "In the south, the Rio Grande do Sul is full of Germans. And the climate isn't tropical—it's cold, it even snows. They have vineyards there—they make excellent wine. You'll see, dear, you'll love it there. And it'll be good for the children."

He tried to encourage her with his reassuring words, but Grete had fallen into depression. She spent hours just flicking through albums of precious old photographs and picture books full of memories. The photograph albums had heavy crimson velvet covers and brass bindings, and each page had small slanted slits to fit the photographs into. The old picture books were packed with pictures, in sepia or dark green tones, showing German landscapes, pretty young blonde girls with carefully arranged plaits and wide smiles, and tall, athletic young men with short-cropped hair, their eyes full of hope, gazing out beyond the horizon.

I used to love browsing through Frau Grete's picture books, particularly the one full of pictures from the Berlin

Olympics. The grand stadium with its flags and banners impressed me enormously. And the athletes—running, jumping, throwing the discus, the javelin. One photograph filled me with pride: the one of old Spyros Louis, who had been enlisted by the Nazi propaganda machine and, proudly sporting the traditional Greek *foustanella*, was pictured receiving a warm handshake from the Führer.

•

Things got worse for Frau Grete after her parents died. First her mother passed away, and then just a few weeks later her father, Karl Schröder, followed her. Grete would spend whole days shut in her room. She did not bother to get dressed, she took no care of herself any more, she just threw a peignoir over her nightdress. She often sat at the piano playing either tender *lieder* or resounding Wagnerian pieces.

It was a couple of years before the paperwork was ready for their departure for Brazil. Olaf went to Cairo to pick up their visas. He was enthusiastic when he got back. "We're all set," he said, as he laid the passports, stamped and signed, on the table. "We're ready to go."

Grete had resigned herself to her fate. They would leave for the New World, but her heart was not in it, she was doing it for the sake of her children. She did not even discuss going to Germany any more, and she never talked of the past.

They started to sell off their things. All their furniture and the piano. Grete wanted to take the gramophone with them. It was an old wind-up His Master's Voice, with a big horn. But Olaf insisted. "What good is it, dear, it's old. We'll buy a new one there, an electric one."

So the gramophone was sold, as were the large porcelain vases and the plaster statues of Negro boys that had stood on either side of the living room door, as if guarding the entrance. Whatever could be packed was put into large wooden cases and sent off to customs. The house was empty. They kept the beds, of course, but even those were sold to the lady downstairs—she would come and collect them when the family had gone.

It was their last night in Alexandria. The children, Brigitte and Karl, teenagers now, were so excited that they could not sleep. They were up by daybreak. They had never traveled by ship before, and although they were sad to leave their friends behind, they were eager to be off.

It was time to go. The children ran ahead to the taxi that waited at the door, each dragging a heavy suitcase behind them. The *bawwab*, Mahmoud, helped with the rest of the bags. Olaf was muttering anxiously to himself. "Yes, I've got the tickets, and the envelope with the money. Where are the passports? Oh, here they are. Come along Grete, dear, let's go, we don't want to be late."

Some of the neighbors had come to see them off.

"Fare you well," said Madame Madeleine, half in French, half in Arabic. "We'll be leaving ourselves next month, our papers have arrived for Australia. Have a good journey, and don't you worry, sweetheart, there's a whole new life waiting for you out there."

Grete looked at her neighbor almost tenderly. She squeezed her hand in both of hers and said, in perfect French, "At my age, Madame Madeleine, one doesn't start a new life, one just goes on living."

She wanted to say more, something nice, to wish her kindly neighbor well, but she was choked by emotion. There was a great lump in her throat. She was on the verge of tears, but it was unseemly for others to see her cry, so she said no more lest she should break down in public. She laid a hand on Madame Madeleine's shoulder, as she cast one last glance around the empty room. The naked walls, with ugly white patches where the pictures and family photographs had hung, where the ghosts of her past had nested.

She must suddenly have realized how attached she was to this apartment, how much she would miss it. She went—almost ran—to the French window, threw it open, and went out onto the balcony—that same corner balcony with the iron railings, the little balcony that looked out over the sea, where, five or six years before, she had so joyfully welcomed the snow. She looked down. The old taxi was laden with their baggage. The children and her husband were waiting outside. The sun was blinding. Her eyes filled with tears. She fumbled in her bag for her sunglasses and put them on.

Frau Grete went back inside, checked her appearance in the reflection of the glass door, straightened her jacket. With a handkerchief, she wiped away a tear that had trickled down her cheek and nestled in the dimple at the side of her mouth. Then she went out onto the landing. She walked steadily down the stairs and out onto the street, where Olaf was waiting for her with a fixed, uncertain smile on his face.

"I'm ready," she said. "Come along, let's go."

Sidi Bishr, October 1942

"We'll leave tomorrow. We're going to Sidi Bishr to stay with Uncle Gaetano." Without any other explanation, my mother announced that we would be leaving our apartment in the center of town and moving to Sidi Bishr, in those days a deserted little village on the coast a few kilometers outside Alexandria. My mother said this with something like relief, as if the decision had been tormenting her for some time, and she added, "Now that your grandmother's passed away, it's best that we leave . . . "

My Italian grandmother, our Nonna, as we called her, had died just two days before.

I can hardly remember Nonna Beatrice. She was very old, small, and thin. She had developed a hunch as she aged, from her arthritis and because of the damp climate of the Great City. She used to sit for hours in her reclining chair, her chaise longue as she called it. Early in the morning, as soon as she awoke, she would drag the old chair, loaded down with cushions, over to the French window that overlooked the balcony. Then she would wait for my mother to come and open the shutters to let the light in, and she would sit there until nightfall.

She neither read, knitted, nor embroidered because, as she put it, her eyes were of no help. She simply looked out onto the street and watched the activity on the sidewalk opposite, the comings and goings on the balconies of the building across the way, and the lazy clouds as they unhurriedly passed across the sky. Occasionally, if I asked her insistently, she would gather up all the strength she had left and tell me a story, stories with characters like Bertoldo and Bertoldino, stories with sly foxes, wicked wolves, evil witches, and kind-hearted mermaids. But she would soon become breathless, she would start to cough, and the story would be left unfinished.

When it was getting dark, as the gas lights in the street below were being lit one by one, Nonna would drag her chair once again to the back of the room. It was in that armchair, among the embroidered cushions, that we found her dead one morning.

"She died like a little bird," my mother said when the aunts and cousins came to pay their last respects.

I was curious to know how little birds die, but as everyone was tearful and dressed in mourning, I hesitated to ask. I tried to solve the question on my own. I began by watching sparrows, but they were happy birds, lively and playful. I would watch them at twilight as they hurriedly gathered in the immense mulberry tree in our back yard. They made such a frenetic noise, as if they were afraid of the oncoming night, as if they feared that the sun would never come out again. And once again I wondered, "What could a little sparrow have to do with Nonna Beatrice?"

I had not the time to come to love my Italian grandmother; she was old and sick and could not compete with my other grandmother, Sarandoula, the Chiot, who was bright and cheerful and chattered like a spinning wheel. Grandma Sarandoula carried within her all the light, optimism and movement of the Aegean. Whenever I was with her she would tell me stories, tales from her childhood in Vrontado.

My Chiot grandmother was jealous of my Italian grandmother, and whenever she talked about her, she called her 'the old woman.'

"How's the old woman?" she would ask, not because she was interested to know about our Nonna's health, but to stress how much younger she was than her. Grandma

Sarandoula was jealous because Nonna Beatrice, my mother's mother, lived with us, while she lived with her cousin Visvikaina, as they were both widows. But another reason why she did not like 'the old woman' was because she was Italian, and Mussolini had invaded Greece two years earlier.

I remember that Grandma Sarandoula taught me a satirical song about Mussolini and she encouraged me to sing it at home.

"To annoy the 'old woman,' the Italian," she told me.

She was so much against both our Nonna and the Duce that at first I thought they must have been related in some way. But as much as I sang, it seemed to have no effect upon either the old Torinesa or my mother.

I did not know that the song was out of date, as the Germans and Italians had already taken Greece. Poor Sarandoula was still living in the victorious days of the Greek campaign in Albania, when "the khaki came and now the Greek flag flies" in Argyrokastro . . . Nobody took any notice of my songs, but when my screeching became annoying my mother would give me a slap and tell me to continue my patriotic exaltations outside, on the back balcony.

•

"Where is Sidi Bishr? Who is Uncle Gaetano?"

These two questions came to me only after the most worrying question: what would become of 'my Thursdays,' which I spent with Grandma Sarandoula? Every Thursday my father took me to the suburb of Sporting, where my Chiot grandmother lived, and I would spend the whole day there. I looked forward to Thursdays. What a good time I used to have with my grandmother. It was a day full of fairy tales, stories, goodies, a day that always ended with pocket money: a shiny, silver half-shilling, which my grandmother would slip discreetly into my trouser pocket as she kissed me goodbye.

I only began to realize why we were leaving the city from

the scattered remarks that were to be heard all around. Everyone was talking anxiously about the advance of the German and Italian troops. Old Theofanis, the baker from Epiros, told us that the Germans had crossed the border and invaded Egypt, that they had reached Marsa Matruh.

"May the hand of God intervene," said the old baker. "Things are looking bad."

It was then that I remembered the words of Osta Antoun, who, as we were fishing the previous Sunday, had whispered, as if not wanting to frighten the fish, "Nothing will stop Rommel. He'll cross the border and in two or three weeks he'll be taking a stroll down the Corniche in Alexandria."

The other fishermen had nodded their heads dourly in agreement. Ismail agreed too. You see, the streets of the Great City had emptied, the Allied troops had left, a sure sign that things had taken a turn for the worse.

Nino, the Yugoslav, who was said to be 'in the know,' whispered that half the troops had gone west to the desert to try to hold Rommel back, while the other half had gone east to hold the canal. And I wondered, "What will become of us without the soldiers?" We had grown used to them; they had become part of our daily life, of the life of the Great City.

"The English have gone," said Nino. "It doesn't look good."

I did not like Nino much, because he was a loudmouth, a big talker with a gross sense of humor, but also because my father had told us to take care—he could be a spy. I asked just how I was supposed to take care, and my father replied, "Just mind what you say . . ."

In Alexandria feelings about the military action in North Africa, which had been going on for months now, were varied and often contradictory. But everyone expected that Rommel would soon enter the city. What would happen? Nobody could answer that question, but everyone wanted to get away from the line of fire while there was still time. The

Egyptians who had nowhere to go tried in whatever way they could to find shelter from the bombardment of the city. They did not much care whether Rommel entered Alexandria, and there were some who secretly wished it.

The Europeans, though, were in a panic. The bombing became more and more intense. The German and Italian bombers were aiming for the port and the army barracks. Slowly the city began to empty.

Until then the Alexandrians, Europeans and locals alike, had lived quietly and peacefully, far from war and con-frontation. The Europeans had lived in the city for two or three generations, some for even longer. With the exception of the events of 1882, when the English warships had bombed the neighborhoods bordering on the Western Harbor, Alexandria and all of Egypt had known many years of peace. Bad news had always come from afar. Battles had been fought elsewhere. Now war was knocking at the door of the Land of the Nile.

"That's the end of our easy days," they said. "The end of the good times."

Other than the Italian and German women and children, who awaited the arrival of the Axis troops as liberators, the Europeans trembled at the thought of a German occupation. Signora Adele called to Kyra Magdalenie as she went off to visit her son, a prisoner of war at the camp in Fayed, "This will be the last time I'll have to make the trip . . . "

Kyra Magdalenie made no reply. Her son was fighting on the front in the desert with the First Greek Brigade. She looked contemptuously at her Italian neighbor and shook her head as if to say, "Just wait and see how well off we'll all be when the Germans get here . . . "

But all the Europeans, even the Italians and the few Germans living in the city, tried to get away from the center. Those who had relatives or friends in Cairo, Tanta, Damanhur, Zagazig, or any of the towns on the canal went there. It was safer in the small cotton-producing towns scattered within the Nile Delta. Those who could, closed up their homes, taking just a few essentials with them, and left. Those who could not leave tried at least to move out of the center of town, to move to the eastern suburbs.

Rommel would enter from the Western Desert, so it would be wise to leave for the east, toward Abu Qir, Rashid, Damietta. There was chaos on the roads and at all the train stations.

"Even bread will be in short supply soon," said Aunt Ione, who kept sending great baking trays with slices of bread off to the baker's to be made into biscuits.

And so we reached the end of June, and a previously unknown name, the name of a small village, was on everyone's lips: El Alamein. El Alamein was some one hundred kilometers from Alexandria. There was a small railway station there. The British and their Allies had decided, at all costs, to stop Rommel at El Alamein, at the gate of Alexandria.

July passed. August came. It was very hot. September followed, then October. The front held. General Montgomery took over from Auchinleck. The Germans and Italians were exhausted but they did not give up. Rommel was immobilized there, but Alexandria was so close—just a few hours away. If he could reach the city, it would change the outcome of the war in North Africa.

It was a narrow front. The sea on one side, the desert and the Qattara Depression on the other. For Rommel to advance, for him to enter Alexandria, he could not go around the depression; he would have to follow the coastal road, he would have to go through El Alamein. But there, the British and their allies had gathered tremendous firepower, and were determined not to retreat. How did they squeeze so many hundreds of tanks, so many thousands of cannons, so many hundreds of thousands of soldiers into such a narrow strip of land? Germans and Italians tried to break through the front. English, Scots, Welsh, Australians and New

Zealanders, Indians, South Africans, Poles, Free French, and Greeks resisted. Each held his weapon tightly, tenaciously in his hands, just as he stubbornly held within him his own sense of what was right. They were all ready, determined, to kill and to die.

The beardless youths were dazed by the brutal sun; they were drunk on the roar of the cannons. They fell endlessly, sometimes prone, sometimes supine, onto the scorched sand, which hungrily sucked their blood. Only the sand knew the whole truth, because she alone touched the burning bodies, tenderly heard their confessions and fondly covered them with her golden dust. She alone knew their last thoughts. To her they entrusted their final jolt of surprise, their last moan. She alone felt the life slithering out of the gaping wounds and gathered drop by drop the murmurs of betrayed dreams: "Why did they lie to us? Why did they tell us that there is a heroic death? A glorious death? They all lied to us, the generals and the priests, even the poets. There is no good death."

•

Sidi Bishr was then a small village on the beach, some fifteen kilometers from the center of town, on the very edge of the desert. A few Alexandrian merchants had put up summer houses there; some were wooden and built close to the sea, and others, which we called villas, were more substantial and were built further inland near to the tram station. The Alexandrians spent their summers in Sidi Bishr and went swimming there. The villas were generally small, two-story houses, very spread out, with the desert stretching out all around. With the *khamsin* wind, great thick clouds of sand blew up, as if trying to expel the intruders, to bury their buildings.

There was very little greenery around. How could plants flourish in such a parched landscape? Just the occasional weary bougainvillea climbing a wall, or a cactus with its despondent, spiky arms resignedly outspread, enduring the torture of the sun. There were, though, many date palms, their tormented trunks standing tall above the endless desert in an effort to hold their heads up high, to peek over the sand dunes and look upon the sea, to cool themselves a little.

It was quite a walk to the sea from the pebbled yard that surrounded Uncle Gaetano's villa. It was very hot that summer and it was hard to walk on the fine, burning sand, which got inside your sandals. But just as you were about to start whining and grumbling about the harsh sun, you would climb that last dune, and there, stretched out before you in all its azure glory, was the Mediterranean.

Sometimes we would go swimming early in the morning, before the sun was high in the sky. The sea was so calm, so peaceful, almost like a painting. Not a ripple marred the mirror-like surface, as if she were weary of the constant movement of the night and had decided to take a rest.

But at night, in the vast silence of the desert, we could hear the sea from a distance. An endless murmur that reached all the way to Uncle Gaetano's 'Villa Felicita.' The sea sighed all night long as the waves came and went one after the other, arriving unhampered from afar, from the open sea, until gently laying themselves down upon the welcoming, sandy shore.

•

Uncle Gaetano and my grandmother Beatrice were first cousins. My uncle was a little old man, good natured and well mannered. I can only just remember him. He was thin, short, with a slight stoop, and had sparse light-gray hair and a snow-white, pointed, little beard.

He always wore a suit and waistcoat, a shirt with a stiffly starched collar, and either a tie or a bow tie. Even on hot summer days, or when the *khamsin* was blowing, Uncle Gaetano never altered his attire. When he went out, he would put on a straw boater with a wide, dark headband and would lean upon his black walking stick with its silver handle in the shape of a duck's head.

They said Uncle Gaetano's son, Enrico, was a soldier. He had volunteered for the Italian army years before, when the Italians were fighting in Abyssinia. Now he was fighting somewhere in North Africa with the Brescia Brigade.

Scattered pieces of news reached my uncle occasionally, unconfirmed rumors. Enrico, they said, had fought at Tobruk, Bardia, Sidi Barrani, and al-Daba. Now he must be fighting in El Alamein.

How long did we stay in Sidi Bishr? A month? Two? Maybe three. I must have been just six years old, and when you are so young it is difficult to judge time; time is of no concern to you, it passes only for others.

The whole of my mother's family had gathered at the Villa Felicita that autumn of 1942. It was a true Tower of Babel.

I do not remember much about the days there. Only a few things come to mind and even those are overshadowed by the beauty of the sea, the sea that both bewitched and terrified me. Perhaps I was afraid of the unknown that the sea hid beneath its immensity, but also perhaps I was frightened because I had heard so much about the 'Devil's Well,' a terrible whirlpool, which, it was said, had swallowed countless young men.

It was Sorial, Aunt Linda's husband, who, in the evenings, told tales of this horrifying sinkhole as well other nightmarish stories of ghosts and vampires. Sorial was a Copt and his Italian was mixed with French and Arabic words.

"Oh, Sorial, stop!" my mother would say. "Leave the ghosts and demons now—it's getting dark. Can't you see that the boy's frightened? He'll have nightmares." And indeed, I was scared by his stories because he was a convincing narrator and he told his tales slowly in a husky, deep voice. But I liked to listen to them. I had a distinct idea about all the creatures from his stories: devils, ghosts, vampires, bogeymen—they were all submerged within the deep well of Sidi Bishr and came out at night as the good Sorial uncorked the magic hole.

Sorial's stories even scared the adults, told as they were at night during the blackout, with the trembling flame of the kerosene lamp casting ghostly shadows.

Although I do not remember much about those days, I recall many small details of the long autumn nights when, after dinner, we would all gather in the large parlor downstairs. The ladies sat in one corner in the dim light, knitting blindly, their metal needles click-clicking together like tiny swords as the women whispered to each other in lowered voices. The three men of the house sat around the main table in the center of the parlor. They smoked. Every evening was the same: Uncle Gaetano looking pensive; my father, sometimes with me upon his knee; Sorial telling his fantastic stories.

Those stories—despite the demons that jumped out at us from the tremulous shadows cast by the flame of the sickly lamp—were a welcome respite from the monotonous accounts of war.

You see, from September of 1940 for two continuous years the Axis troops and the Allied forces had been going back and forth on the coastal strip of desert from Tunisia to Cyrenaica. Attack, counterattack, followed invariably by the counting of the dead and wounded, those missing in action or taken prisoner.

Montgomery set the commencement of a massive attack for late in the evening of October 23. The night was cold, as it often is in the desert, and above shone the unmerciful light of the moon. Sorial said that Montgomery had purposely chosen that night because it suited his plans.

One thousand two hundred Allied cannons thundered all night long, and all the next day, and the third day, and the fourth day without pause, and the fifth day and the sixth. October passed, November came, and the cannons continued to spew out burning iron, hatred, and death. Twelve days and nights of fire. The Germans and Italians held their

ground, returned fire, and did not retreat.

News of the great battle reached Alexandria with lightning speed. In Sidi Bishr every evening just after nightfall, the three men of the Villa Felicita, the Italian, the Copt, and the Greek, would climb silently up onto the terrace to survey the horizon. The gentle breeze brought only the sound of the sea, indifferent to the evil of man. But there, far away beyond the darkness, you could see flashes of light over the great battle.

"The desert is boiling," Uncle Gaetano said one evening, and his two companions nodded their heads.

Night after night they climbed up onto the darkened terrace and sat on makeshift stools, their elbows resting upon the stone wall, their eyes turned toward El Alamein, waiting.

Most of the time they were silent, rapt in their own thoughts. Few words were exchanged—and those in undertones, expecting no reply.

"The fire seems more intense to me tonight," my father said. "They're getting closer."

Silence.

"It's getting late," said Sorial. "They won't bomb Alexandria tonight—all the planes are at the front."

Silence again.

"Don't worry. It'll be all right," said my father. He said it so quietly that he could only just be heard.

At that moment, an owl shrieked, its melancholy voice seeming to contradict him.

"Bad omen," said Sorial nervously.

"The voice of death," said Uncle Gaetano. "Who's she crying for, I wonder?"

All was quiet again for a long time. The owl, having seen the men, was startled and flew away in low, heavy, and silent retreat.

The stars twinkled in the clear sky. Suddenly a star fell, shooting across the sky like a firework.

"I wonder where Enrico is?" murmured Uncle Gaetano, wishing on the falling star.

Sorial realized that the question was not directed at him, but he felt the need to say something. He wanted in some way to soften his father-in-law's pain, but he could not find the right words of comfort. He sighed and said, "God is great . . ."

He said this in Arabic, because although he spoke many languages, some expressions came to him best in that language.

All was silent again.

•

On November 4, the German–Italian front was broken and the retreat began. It was the beginning of the end of the war in North Africa. We stayed in Sidi Bishr for a while longer before returning to our apartment in town.

•

I never saw Uncle Gaetano again. We learned that Enrico had fought at El Alamein, was wounded and taken prisoner, but eventually returned to Alexandria. Ever since then, I had wanted to see El Alamein, to visit the site of the legendary battle that had forced us to leave our home and move to Sidi Bishr.

The years passed. It must have been 1950 or 1951 before I managed to go to El Alamein for the first time. It was still a wild place then, still vividly reminiscent of that clash of the titans. The impressive monuments with which each side honored their dead had not yet been erected. The landscape was still. Thousands of crosses standing up all over, and around them the beasts of war rusting powerless among the endless minefields. You could still read the faded signs: *Achtung, Minenfeld*.

I set out toward the sea to cool down a little, to escape the midday sun and the weight of death that hung all around. I climbed the low sand dunes that looked out over the sea. They reminded me of Sidi Bishr. I felt nostalgic for those days of innocence when my only fear was of the Devil's Well and

Sorial's simple, harmless stories.

I looked at the sea—the same sea as in Sidi Bishr, aquamarine—and drank in its vastness. Suddenly, a little way off to my left on a slight elevation, I saw a ramshackle building, a single small room with a low, whitewashed wall around it. I thought it must have been a military observation post.

Something was written on the wall. I tried to make it out, but time had almost erased the message. I was curious, so I went closer and managed with difficulty to read the words, written in large capital letters with black paint that had faded in some places. And it read in Italian: "We were not lacking in courage but fate decided otherwise."

I still remember that cry of despair of the unknown soldier, that conscript who, before abandoning his post, had felt the need to justify his action to the generations to come, to explain why he had not died.

The Three Brothers

Before the war there may have been more monks at our school, but by the 1940s there were only three of them left. They were all French, belonged to the Order of Saint Jean-Baptiste de la Salle, and had dedicated their lives to the education of the young.

Frère Léon was the headmaster. He was a nice, quiet man. With his long white beard and imposing bearing, he looked rather like one of those revered patriarchal characters, as if he had emerged from the pages of our religious schoolbook. He had a slight stoop and tended to shuffle when he walked. He must have been very old, but his eyes refused to age. Like some final bastion of youth, they seemed to retain all that remained of the tenacious flame of life, which refused to be extinguished.

He no longer taught, but busied himself with the administration of the school. He had come to Alexandria from France at the end of the previous century. They used to say jokingly that he was the same age as many of our schoolbooks—they were all ancient editions. And yet, back then, things seemed to mature more gently with time. There was no great hurry. You could leisurely savor the essence of an old book. A book written in 1920 was still current in 1940 or 1945, and still useful at the beginning of the 1950s.

We did not see much of Frère Léon. He rarely came into our classrooms and we had no business being anywhere near his office. But he used to come to ceremonies and sports events and to the celebrations of the beginning and end of term, occasions when the whole school would gather in the great hall.

At the beginning of the academic year I used to go with my father to enroll at the school. We would go into the office of the headmaster, the Très Cher Frère Directeur. The 'Très Cher' was an addition to his title that showed his high standing in the brotherhood. The other monks were addressed simply as Cher Frère. Every year I remember my father haggling over the exorbitant cost of school fees. "The boy's a good pupil, he's intelligent, and he likes French," he would insist, adding that it would be a shame if he had to take me out of the French school and send me to the Greek Community School, which was also very good . . . and charged no fees whatsoever. Then he would stress that he personally preferred the French religious schools because they gave the children a good Christian education and helped to start them out on the right road in life.

Frère Léon appeared quite moved. He would cross his small, plump hands across his chest, half close the cunning little eyes that sparkled behind his glasses, and put forward his own case in defense of the steep fees. "Have you any idea how much it costs just to maintain this school?"

He would slap his palm to his forehead as if suddenly feeling dizzy. "Ah! ah! ah! ah!" he would exclaim, in such distress that at first I used to feel guilty—as if the school were being kept open purely for my sake. As far as my father's claims were concerned, Frère Léon agreed absolutely, of course; I had jumped a year—I had gone straight from the first grade to the third—but he had to point out that I was a naughty child. Once he got a bit carried away and said I was "a little devil." However, he regretted this reference to Satan, and, after crossing himself copiously, he devoutly kissed the silver cross that hung around his neck in stark contrast to his austere black cassock.

The good brother did not fail to point out also that this was a Catholic school, and was therefore obliged to give priority to Catholic pupils, for whom the fees were considerably lower, almost nominal. My father, pretending not to understand the insinuation of the shrewd monk, added thoughtfully: "But we are all Christians, are we not?"

For as long as I knew him, Frère Léon was always unwell, and rumors were rife that he was to be replaced. Frère Louis, the youngest of the three monks, had been considered the most likely successor, but there was talk of a new brother being sent out from France to assume the post as soon as the war ended. I was a little afraid of Frère Léon, particularly when he frowned and tried to look severe.

•

My favorite brother was Frère Jean-Baptiste, the eldest of the three monks. They said he was ten years older than Frère Léon, but that must have been an exaggeration. Frère Jean-Baptiste also had a patriarchal air. He was extremely tall, portly, yet not fat, and he walked with a slow, noble stride. With his white beard reaching down to his waist, he was the spitting image of Abraham in the lithograph that hung in our classroom. But it was the eyes that stood out from Jean-Baptiste's face: they were the color of the calm sky and quite transparent. They gazed out at you with a good-natured smile and drew you straight into his soul.

To me, Frère Jean-Baptiste was something akin to an ancient monument, a monument that carried with it the history of the century past. Despite the years that lay heavily upon him, he continued to teach—he gave scripture and music classes—but he was also the school organist, accompanying the hymns at every service.

I was very fond of Frère Jean-Baptiste—he was like a grandfather to me. He never lost his temper; he never punished us. When we went a bit too far and he had to put his foot down, he did not raise his voice or whack his ruler angrily on the desk like the other teachers did. He simply had to stand up and look around the class with a frown, and we would calm down immediately. Then the good brother would sit down again, his face resuming its customary good-natured expression.

Sometimes Frère Jean-Baptiste would let me stand next to him when he was playing the organ and he would show me which stops to pull out. I was not very interested in music and my knowledge of tonic sol–fa went no further than do, re, mi—but I enjoyed helping him. It made me feel proud, as if I were doing something important.

I may not have been a music lover, but I enjoyed the songs Frère Jean-Baptiste taught us. The most popular song among the younger children was "Frère Jacques." Somehow, I came to associate the Frère Jacques of the well-known song, who rang out the bells *ding dang dong* every morning, with Frère Jean-Baptiste, even though it was not he who rang the school bell to tell us to go into class or to go out to play. Once, instead of declaring that Frère Jean-Baptiste was coming down the corridor, I shouted, "Hey, here comes Frère Jacques!" And after that the nickname stuck.

But I am forgetting the most important part—Frère Jean-Baptiste was the school librarian, and from the third grade I was already his assistant. For me, the school library held a special attraction. It was a mysterious place, where the initiation to knowledge began.

It was not particularly large, but it was my first library, and so will always hold a special place in my heart, even when I compare it to the extensive and imposing libraries I came to know later in life. For me, that first school library was my first love, which is, as they say, never forgotten.

The library was on the ground floor, with one door giving out onto the schoolyard and another onto the corridor leading to the classrooms. It was just one spacious room, but much bigger than a classroom. It was dark in there, because the large window that overlooked the schoolyard was always kept closed, its heavy curtains drawn so that the sounds of children playing should not intrude upon that oasis of silence and disturb the concentration of those within.

The books were set out in long rows upon wooden shelves that ran around the room, covering all four walls. They started off low down, near the planked wooden floor, and climbed right up to the ceiling, where they kept company with an army of spiders.

Frère Jean-Baptiste could reach the books on the lower shelves, but it was quite impossible for him to climb the ladder and reach those higher up. That was my job. But the librarian also assigned me to more important duties, like checking the library cards of borrowed books and replacing returned books to their proper places. I must admit that we did not have much work to do, as few children bothered to take books out. The library was open only during break time, so it was not particularly popular.

The old librarian sat behind a large oak desk on a low wooden platform in a corner of the room. There were always piles of books around him and an open book in front of him. He would settle down with the intention of reading, placing a book under the glow of the overhead light with its large green Bakelite shade, but watching from my corner I would notice that sometimes, instead of reading, his eyes would be following the electric cable that ran from high up on the spider-filled ceiling and continued down, down, on its perpetual path until it reached almost to the desk.

Frère Jean-Baptiste often fell asleep in his chair. His was not the treacherous sleep that creeps up upon the aged, but a deliberate sleep, the welcome sleep of one who knows that his conscience is clear: all is well with himself, with those around him, and with God. When he was ready to sleep Frère Jean-Baptiste would take off his spectacles with their delicate wire frames and put them in their silver case, which he would place carefully on the edge of the desk. He would fold his hands across his chest, lean back in his chair, settle himself down comfortably and take a nap. Sleep would come at once, and in just a few moments a loud snoring could be heard. Frère Jean-Baptiste slept the sleep of the just, like children do before being burdened with original sin, because he too communicated with the angels, with the primitive God.

The assistant librarian's post—my post, that is—was a simple oak table, quite large, set in the opposite corner, with an imposing old leather-upholstered armchair.

It is difficult to describe the smell of our library. How do you describe the smell of time? It is not hard to describe the fragrance of flowers; there are countless adjectives to capture the scent of spring, the salty tang brought by the sea, the aroma of a pie slowly baking in an Egyptian oven. The Great City was enveloped by so many smells; they could be identified, classified, and described in simple words and they could be made into poems and songs. But it is no easy task to describe the smell of a book aging peacefully on a wooden shelf in the half-light of an old library. Each has its own scent. It differs according to the quality, the thickness of the paper, the dampness it has absorbed, the years it has remained unopened, unhappy, with dust settling upon it, its leather-backed spine slowly rotting. I learned to tell the books apart by their smell, like a wine expert sniffs a wine before he tastes it.

There were no new books in the library; they were all quite old, mostly from the previous century. Once I heard Frère Jean-Baptiste grumbling, "A library which is not enriched dies." There were a lot of novels, a fair number of religious books, others on history and travel, there were atlases and periodicals . . . Most were in French, with the few exceptions of some in English and Latin.

Standing impressively on one shelf, bound in red with gold lettering, were the works of Jules Verne. Further along, those of Racine, Rabelais, the tales of La Fontaine, the tender stories of Hector Malot, and the writings of la Comtesse de Ségur next to those of Charles Dickens, Hans Christian Andersen, and the Brothers Grimm.

On another shelf, set apart, were books relating the great explorations. I was fascinated by them. They described the adventures of the French, English, and Belgians and their endeavors to colonize distant lands. Most of these adventures unfolded on the Dark Continent. The European 'heroes' fought with cross or sword in hand—often with both—flying in the face of danger, to overcome wild beasts and man-eating natives in remote virgin forests. Others crossed vast deserts, battling with the terrible Tuareg. Mythical names: Timbuktu, Fashoda, Brazzaville, Stanleyville—and all this so that they could raise a flag and erect a cross . . . Others fought for the honor of France— offended by the Bey of Algeria when he slapped the unfortunate French ambassador with his fan—and conquered whole countries, turning them into France d'Outre-mer.

The illustrations in these books inclined you to take the part of the honorable European officer who, on horseback or mounted upon a camel, aimed his long-barreled rifle at his cruel adversary, while the grisly, wild native, having just polished off some poor white soldier, stood half-naked and goggle-eyed, with human skulls piled up around his hut. The bearer of civilization himself was no angelic character. His eyes were set upon killing, but he, at least, was clothed; and nearby stood a standardbearer carrying a drum, or more often a cross-bearing clergyman to bring the path of Christ to any savage who should escape the carnage.

Personally, I took neither side. Of course, I could not side with the savages, because they were not Christians, but neither could I support the obligatory 'salvation' that the white man was attempting to impose. When I tried to discuss this with the good librarian, I hesitatingly asked him whether Christ had not also come for the salvation of the cannibals. In response, he spoke to me of love and the equality of all men in the eyes of the Lord, and then closed the book with its blood-soaked pictures, as if to renounce it.

There were many books I wanted to read but which were

not stocked in our library, like those of Alexandre Dumas, Victor Hugo, Prosper Mérimée, Leo Tolstoy, Dostoyevsky, and others. I never asked myself why these books were missing, but I dreamed of someday owning them.

•

Frère Louis was the third brother in our school. He was different in every way from the other brothers. He was much younger, for a start—forty-five at most. I remember him as being slight of build, short, with a rounded, moon-shaped, cleanshaven face, which was somewhat sallow and expressionless. He had sparse dark hair, which he took great care to comb in such a way as to make it cover his bald head. He walked quickly, almost at a trot, and all his gestures were nervous. He rarely smiled. When he did smile, it did not seem to suit his face.

The older pupils, who concerned themselves with school gossip, said that Frère Louis would soon succeed Frère Léon as headmaster. It seemed likely, as the diminutive monk had already taken on that puffed-up air of superiority that the ambitious adopt when they believe that their time has come to savor power.

Frère Louis taught us arithmetic, algebra, and geometry. I have often wondered if that is why I never took a liking to numbers and am not much good at calculations. He was very strict with us and imposed severe punishments for the slightest misconduct. Whenever I passed outside a classroom and heard a ruler being whacked across a desk, I always thought, "That's him . . . " But Frère Louis not only struck his ruler across desktops; he also used it to inflict punishment upon his pupils. Like all my classmates, I had felt the harsh hand of Frère Louis and his outdated idea of discipline.

It was not difficult to receive ten, fifteen, or even twenty whacks with the ruler from Frère Louis. Simple childish mischief or teasing would suffice. We came to realize that the intensity of the punishment could be reduced by crying out

at the first strokes, so most children began wailing as soon as the ruler was raised, before it even reached the palm of the outstretched hand. Woe betide those who refused to cry . . .

I tried not to cry, or at least not to let Frère Louis see me cry. Lopez, the Spaniard I shared a desk with, did the same. Lopez used to say he was going to be a bullfighter when he grew up, and matadors do not cry. I thought: "Lopez is right; he is right to take a caning silently because he will be famous one day in Spain, but I have no such ambitions, so why should I tempt the wrath of little Brother Ludwig?"

The thrashing was much more severe for those who did not cry out, howl, and beg for mercy. Whack! Fifteen, sixteen, seventeen . . . Frère Louis really put his back into it and took out all his spite upon us. In rabid fury he raised and brought down the ruler, breathlessly counting each stroke out loud, while I imagined him saying to himself, "Take *that*—because I hate you all. Take *that*—because I was born short. And take *that*—because I am ugly. And take *that*—because I have denied myself so much . . . and eighteen and nineteen and twenty . . . "

When he was done, he would tumble exhausted into his chair, worn out, while his victim continued to prance around spitting on his palms to soothe the stinging. I must admit, though, that a caning from Frère Louis was always well orga-nized—the other teachers just gave us the odd slap or tug on the ear in the heat of the moment.

But the ruler was not the only means of punishment for naughty pupils. For lesser offenses you could be made to stand in the corner of the classroom, staring stupidly at the wall for an hour or so. Or you could be kept in at break—you had to stay in the classroom alone while the others were out playing—or you could be forced to copy out lines, fifty, a hundred, or two hundred times: "I will not bring a cat into the classroom again. I will not bring a cat into the classroom again. I will not . . . " I once spent a whole Sunday writing this same phrase over and over again, but it did not reduce my love for the cute four-legged creatures, nor did it prevent me from devising new and mischievous pranks.

Another form of punishment was the striking of 'bons points' as a last resort. This was almost equal to a thrashing and was imposed by all the members of staff because it was convenient and effective, without making the teacher unnecessarily unpopular.

'Bons points' were 'good marks'—small colored pieces of cardboard, like coupons, with the signature of the headmaster stamped on them, which pupils received as a reward for good behavior, commendable results in exams or team sports, or progress in a particular subject. But most importantly, these colored coupons could be used to 'buy off' some other punishment—depending upon the offense, of course.

You would hear Monsieur Chehéb, the Lebanese teacher who taught us French, and who was lenient in his punishments, say, "So that Alonso may learn to pay attention in class and stop gaping at the pigeons outside the window, he will write fifty times the line: 'I will not stare at the pigeons during class.' Or he may buy back that punishment with two bons points."

•

That is how we spent the years of the Second World War. Bombs rained down by night, punishments by day, all mixed up with songs, games, lessons, childish mischief. It seems that the war did not cause us any serious upset at school. The heavy bombing that went on until 1942 began to die down, but because of the war neither new monks nor new books arrived from occupied France.

Frère Louis was impatient to be made headmaster. Frère Léon insisted on maintaining his post to the bitter end . . . while Frère Jean-Baptiste, untroubled by it all, enjoyed the tranquillity of those who expect nothing. He continued to concern himself with good, simple things: music, books, the children, the Church, and the good Lord.

War's end brought little change to things at school. The first illustrated periodicals began to appear on the news-stands—we had not seen a French magazine since 1939—and a little later, I think in 1947, a new children's publication came out featuring the adventures of that amiable hero Tin-Tin and his lively dog Milou. I could not have imagined as I held that first issue in my hands that that bright young lad with the shocking forelock of hair would enjoy fame throughout the next half century.

After the end of the war, the first chocolates and other goodies, and gradually toys, began to appear in the shop windows.

•

I reached the final year of junior school. I had completed my first six years of education. For the following six, I would have to choose between Saint Mark's College—a well-known Catholic school—and the equally good high school run by the French state.

That year, a new monk arrived from France to take up the post of headmaster. The young Très Cher Frère Antoine must have been under thirty. He was German. Why they sent us a German monk immediately following the war, I had no idea. But it did not bother us much, nor was it discussed at school.

He was a good-looking blond youth, tall, with a thin, gentle face, and he wore gold-framed glasses. He spoke French with a slight accent. We called him German, but thinking back now, I suppose he might have been French from Alsace or Lorraine.

With the arrival of Frère Antoine came a breath of fresh air. The new headmaster was always on the move; he was every-where at once. He was simple, smiling, he talked to the children, and, unbelievable as it was, he even joined in our games from time to time.

One day when we were playing football, he appeared in the playground and asked if he could play. "Yeah!" cheered the children. "Yeeeeeeah!" So he joined in, and when he got the ball he deftly hitched up his cassock with one hand and began to dribble it with a skill that left us all speechless. He passed through the whole of the opposing team's defense and, like an ace, scored one goal after another.

The whole school marveled at the athletic prowess of the new headmaster.

Frère Louis was most put out. He became more and more bad-tempered and never missed an opportunity to show his disapproval of the new-fangled vices the young headmaster was introducing. But of course, he had taken a vow of obedience, so he could do nothing to change matters; he just had to accept them. It was obvious, though, that he felt he had been wronged. Not only had he been passed over as headmaster, but the person who had been given that enviable post was a mere youngster, a revolutionary, and on top of that, he had a German accent.

Frère Louis became more irritable by the day, with outbursts of temper often bordering on hysteria.

•

Frère Léon did not return to France, but, we learned, had asked his superiors to allow him to die in Alexandria, in his school. He rarely left his small apartment, and had difficulty in dragging his swollen legs along.

One day, before the end of the school year, there was a celebration of some sort, and he came into the hall. Weary from the effort, he collapsed into an armchair that had been placed in his honor in the front row. My father went to greet him; he told him they had not met for a long time; he asked about his health, made general conversation.

"Oh, my good friend," Frère Léon replied when he recognized my father, "what a difficult thing it is to die . . . !"

But nonetheless, the old headmaster lived for many more years. He was still alive ten years later when I left Egypt.

•

It was the last day of term, my last day at that school. I knew I had passed the year. I was happy—the summer holidays were ahead. I would never return to that school, but I felt no nostalgia, no regret at losing so many friends.

There were no lessons on the last day of term. There was a ceremony with poems, songs and awards. But there was something even more important for us on that last day: it was time to redeem our bons points. A row of prizes was set out in the classroom, religious trinkets mostly—crucifixes and crosslets, icons, prayer beads, statuettes of the Virgin and other plaster saints.

So that no one should be left out, there were books, pencil cases, crayons, and exercise books for the non-Catholics— half of my classmates were Jews, Muslims, and Orthodox Christians. Each item bore a label stating its value in bons points. With two bons points you could get a packet of colored chalk; with three, an exercise book; with four a coloring book or a cross. With five bons points you could get a storybook or some prayer beads. The more colored coupons, the better the prize.

Looking back now, I cannot imagine that my classmates and I have ever since savored such pleasure as that which we enjoyed on receiving those simple objects. I had managed to gather nineteen bons points. I was a naughty boy—I had never managed to get so many before. I always won them on the one hand, and lost them on the other as repayment for my mischief. My bons points never lasted long.

I was quite amazed myself at how many I had managed to collect—I counted and recounted the colored coupons that I had stored in an empty cigarette tin. In just a few minutes, the process of exchanging bons points for prizes would begin. All the children had gathered around the table where the prizes were on show, each of us calculating what we could claim. I was impressed by a beautiful wooden cross standing on a black plaster base. The plaster Christ on the cross, wearing a hopeless expression, gazed up at the heavens. *That's* what I want, I said to myself.

And then the teachers arrived to get the proceedings started—Frère Louis, the Maltese history teacher, and another member of the staff who I cannot remember now. There was a lot of noise in the class, as if we were all trying to get in one last bit of mischief and japery before the end of the school year.

"Quiet!" shouted Frère Louis in his squeaky voice as he banged his ruler irritably against the desk. Reluctantly the children calmed down, but three or four of us exchanged the last nudge and giggle of the last day of the last class. At that moment, Bogos, the Armenian, made a sound like a cat: just as the class fell silent a loud *miaoooow* was heard. We all fell about laughing.

Whatever made him do it? Frère Louis was livid, and because he could not make out who it was who had made the sound, he called the three naughtiest pupils out—the Maltese boy in front of me, the Italian standing next to me, and me—and he took away two bons points from each of us. "There goes my beautiful cross," I thought, because I was now down to seventeen coupons. I would have to look for another prize.

I tried to protest to the sallow-faced monk. I assured him that it was not me who had made the noise. I explained—and I think that was my mistake—that if I lost those two bons points I would not be able to claim the cross that I had set my heart on. He was surprised. "Why, how did *you* manage to get so many bons points?"

I was about to show him my coupons when he said, "Tell me who played the cat, and I won't take any of your bons points away."

I continued to assure him that it was not me, but insisted that I could not tell him who it was. He began to take away my bons points—one for every question I left unanswered.

"Who did it?"

"I don't know."

Sixteen bons points left.

"Who made that noise?"

"I don't know."

Fifteen bons points.

When I was down to ten, he still kept asking, "Who made the cat noise?" and in desperation I shouted, "I won't tell you!" Frère Louis went even paler than usual, his hands began to shake, and he grabbed all my bons points. I just stood there holding the open, empty cigarette tin.

I wanted to protest, I wanted to make him see how unfair he was being, but every time I tried to open my mouth I thought I would burst into tears. I did not want to cry; I knew how much satisfaction that would give him. But how could I not cry? I was so easily moved.

The classroom was dead quiet. Frère Louis was still standing there in silence, uneasily holding in his hands the colored coupons he had deprived me of. I gathered all my strength with great effort, forced back my tears, and blurted out: "It's not fair! You're a wicked man. God will punish you."

The words came out in a loud rush, so that they would not be drowned by tears. I could not stand any more. I threw open the door and ran out into the corridor. There the tears finally overflowed. I followed the long, dark corridor and slowly started down the great stairway.

As I went down the stairs sobbing, I met Frère Jean-Baptiste. When he saw me, he clucked his tongue in disapproval as he did when he wished to criticize without using words. "Tut tut tut. Why so sad, my little Greek?" That was his pet name for me, as I was the only Greek, and the smallest in the class.

There on the stairs, I poured out my grievances and told him what had happened. It did me good to get it off my chest. It calmed not only my tears but also the angry indignation I felt. It was as if there were a volcano inside me that had erupted, and as the lava flowed out so my distress and tears overflowed. I told him everything, the whole story.

When I got to the part where I had called Frère Louis wicked and unfair, Frère Jean-Baptiste frowned and made that drawn out tutting sound again. Then he dipped his hand deep into his pocket and brought out a bunch of keys, selected the key to the library, gave it to me and said: "Go and wash your face, and then wait for me in the library."

Soon I was alone in the library. I had never been in there all on my own before. I began to browse along the shelves, idly reading the titles. I tried to wipe the episode with Frère Louis from my mind, to recover my wits, to calm down among my beloved books. A long time passed and Frère Jean-Baptiste had not returned. It was almost time for the bell to ring, the bell which would announce the end of the day, the end of the year, the end of an era.

I began to worry. What was taking him so long? Had the incident with Frère Louis brought repercussions? I ought to go upstairs and get my bag, which I had left at my desk. My report card was in it, my school certificate—the certification that I had completed my basic education. What if Frère Louis had contrived to take it away from me? What if I had to repeat the same class? I knew it was impossible, but I said to myself, "Who knows what a mean man like him could do?"

Suddenly the library door opened and Frère Jean-Baptiste came in with his slow, noble stride. He sat down at his desk and gestured for me to come closer. Then I noticed that he was carrying a cross and a book. He looked over the top of his spectacles, letting them slide down his nose as he did when he wanted to examine something closely.

"You see," he said, as if we were continuing some interrupted conversation, "we Catholics have the advantage of regular confession. So whosoever should slip into transgression may unburden himself, repent, and feel so much better for the forgiveness of his sins. You, of course, have confessed your sin—you should not have spoken so harshly to Frère Louis. I am not your confessor to pardon you, but I know you are sorry. Two wrongs do not make a right. And Frère

Louis, who has dedicated his life to the education of children, cannot be either an unfair or a wicked person. One day you'll understand all this. God sees all. I've brought you this cross, so that you may pray for God to grant you humility and tolerance. Take it, it's yours to remember me by."

He also gave me a book—*Le Petit Prince* by Saint-Exupéry.

Just then, the bell rang and all the children rushed out of the classrooms. We always did that when the bell rang, but this was the very last day of the school year and the stampede was even more frantic, the dash down the stairs more boisterous, the chattering merrier.

It was silent in the library but for the sound of a horsefly trapped behind the curtains, banging repeatedly against the windowpane as it tried to escape.

I felt my eyes filling up with tears again. I wanted to thank Frère Jean-Baptiste, but it seemed my lips were stuck tightly together and I could not get any words out. So I leaned over the desk and grasped the thick black penholder which stood there next to the inkwell. I hurriedly dipped the pen in the ink and scribbled on a sheet of paper that was sticking out from the piles of old books on the desk: *Merci Frère Jacques . . .* then I turned and ran out.

Athinodoros and Iordanis

The office was run by English standards. The owner, Mr.
Athinodoros G. Pervanidis, had lived for many years in
Liverpool. He had started out young in the great English
port working for a leading shipping company. Gradually,
with hard work, he had been promoted to supervisor of the
accounting department and later, when the company took
on a Greek partner, Pervanidis was made general manager.
When he was over sixty years old, at an age when most are
retiring, Mr. Athinodoros decided to set up his own business. He returned to Alexandria, the city of his birth, and
opened a shipping office, the Ath. G. Pervanidis Shipping
Agency.

At the Pervanidis Agency everything ran with the meticu-
lousness characteristic of its founder. Let us begin with the
office itself: outside the front door of 36 Rue Nabi Daniel,
among the brass plaques bearing the names of the other
firms in the building, that of the Ath. G. Pervanidis Shipping
Agency stood out not only because of its freshly polished
sheen, but also because of a distinctive, unadorned austerity.
The letters were engraved in calligraphic script filled in with
black enamel. Easily discernible even from a distance, without being either too large or too small. The name was written
in English only, plain and simple, nothing else other than a
note of the floor—*1er étage*—written in French. The plaque,
firmly fixed to the wall on its varnished oak frame, conjured
up an image of refined splendor.

When you climbed the two or three marble steps leading

from the sidewalk to the entrance, you found yourself in a large, attractive space. The floor was laid with multicolored marble slabs. To the right, hanging on a yellowed wall, were miscellaneous signs informing the visitor of the offices that operated within the four stories of the *okella*. All of the first floor was rented by Mr. Athinodoros. The other floors housed various shipping companies, a Coptic lawyer, and a well-known French cotton merchant.

In the middle of the opposite wall there was a large niche that held a plaster statue of Diana. It seems it was a copy of an inelegant Roman work, heavily decorated with eastern additions, depicting the goddess as plump, half-naked, and dusty. She greeted the visitor with a bored expression and seemed to follow him out of the corner of her eye as he walked to the lift or to the foot of the staircase.

The lift was Viennese. Spacious, made of solid wood and artistically worked wrought iron, it resembled a large cage. Although you could hear it groaning and squeaking as it solemnly passed from one floor to another, it gave a feeling of stability and security.

But you could get to the first floor more quickly on foot. Halfway up the stairs, in another small niche, you met another statue. I do not remember what it was exactly, some sort of Ptolemaic god, a cross between Hellenistic elegance and Oriental mysticism.

Despite the grandeur of the entrance hall, you could sense decline. But then, at the beginning of the 1950s, that was how things were with all the buildings in Alexandria. You could no longer make out what the original color of their walls had been. You looked at a surface and thought, "Years ago, that wall must have been white or gray." Now the colors were uncertain, grubby, grimy, and dingy. The plaster was swollen with the dampness that enshrouded the city. There were cracks in the walls and yawning gaps where the plaster had flaked off, like unhealed wounds revealing great stones and bricks: the bowels of the building. The perceptive passer-by

felt that the Great City, the famed Alexandria of Egypt, was gasping her dying breath.

Nobody worried about maintenance and decorating during the uncertain years between the wars and the difficult ones that followed the Second World War. Gradually the process had begun that would slowly, unhurriedly, transform the buildings into beautiful ruins.

At number 36 Rue Nabi Daniel, there were countless examples of dereliction. The chandeliers in the entrance hall had lost half of their light bulbs and many of their ornate, Bohemian crystal drops that had once shone like tiny stars. The marble on the floor was shabby, as were the steps, which were worn down at the edges. Some of the windowpanes were cracked and others were missing completely. The brass stair-rods lay uselessly upon the stairs, orphaned, vainly waiting for a thick, purple stair-carpet to be laid. These and many other details, together with the strong smell of mildew, testified to past grandeur.

Mr. Athinodoros saw all this and was unhappy about the decline of the *okella*, the decline of the city. But the owner, Mahmoud Bey, was not to be moved. Mahmoud Bey had arrived in Alexandria from the country and had bought the grand old *okella* from a Jew with the money he got from selling an *ezba* in Tanta. At the end of every month, accompanied by Masoud, the building administrator—a slimy, wretched man—Mahmoud Bey arrived to collect the rent. But he was not about to spend a single penny on maintenance of the building.

"Whoever doesn't like it can leave," he said one day with a calm, confident expression, lifting up the hem of his white *gallabiya*, which dragged on the floor. In this way, he cut short the complaints made by the Coptic lawyer about the unacceptable state of the building.

But let us return to the staircase; we had reached the first floor, in front of the big oak door where you came once again upon the words 'Ath. G. Pervanidis Shipping

Agency' engraved upon yet another shiny brass plaque.

Abduh, the oldest of the three office boys, was responsible for the polishing of all the plaques, not just the ones I have mentioned. There was a brass sign on each of the doors in the office. Some were engraved in Greek, in large capital letters: Management, Agency, Accounts Department, Cargo Department, Teller, Archives. Poor Abduh, a bulky Nubian with a black face that shone like ebony, invariably had a duster in his hand and was always polishing: plaques, doorknobs, window handles, hinges, light switches. The office was full of brass and Mr. Athinodoros wanted it all immaculate.

As soon as you passed through the front door, you entered another world, as if leaving behind the misery and dilapidation of the present and stepping into a bygone world of well-kept neatness and elegance. You had entered the world of Mr. Athinodoros Pervanidis.

Mr. Athinodoros was meticulous, obsessed with order and cleanliness, a real stickler for correctness and form, for order and punctuality. He himself arrived at the office every day at exactly eight o'clock. He was a small man, and thin. In the winter he wore a dark suit with a double-breasted waistcoat, a white shirt with stiffly starched collar and cuffs and shiny gold cufflinks. His tie was always dark, tied in a large knot, and a white handkerchief peeked out of his breast pocket. A hat was indispensable—a gray homburg in the winter, but in the summer, when he wore a white linen suit, he replaced this with a light panama. The finishing touches to Mr. Athinodoros' appearance were his shiny black shoes and a smart walking cane with its silver handle. He did not lean on the cane, because despite his years—he must have been almost eighty—he walked well, erect, proud, with a sure step and head held high. It seems he thought the cane to be a necessary accessory to his careful appearance.

The hierarchy of the office was strict. Unquestioned, at the top, the 'master' was Mr. Athinodoros, as he liked to be called, rather than Mr. Pervanidis. But the 'Mr.' differed from the normal use of the word; it was mister with a capital M, something like the term 'Lord' when used by a God-fearing believer referring to the Creator. We used to say 'Mr. Athinodoros' in a particular way, the tongue moving slowly around the words, syllable by syllable, as if they filled the mouth, while the face took on an appropriate expression of respect. 'Athinodoros' sounded much like a form of address reserved for speaking to a ruler, a lord, a holy father, as if it should have been followed by the title 'the Great.'

When a member of the staff wanted to know if Mr. Athinodoros was in his office, he would discreetly ask one of the office boys who stood outside. Alternatively, he could ask Mr. Athinodoros' driver, Mr. Kleanthis, who was always to be found pacing the corridors at the ready—you never could tell when, without warning, the boss might decide to pop down to the port to oversee the loading of a ship, or when he might suddenly wish to drop in on the manager of the Ottoman Bank.

In a corner of the hallway, high on the wall, was a flat box, something like a bell board, with small metal squares on it. On each square there was a number. This was the inter-office communications system—rudimentary but effective. Each number corresponded to a department supervisor. Number 1 was for Mr. Lefteris, who was in charge of the accounting department, number 2 for Mr. Alekos in charge of the agency, and so on. The office boys had a number too, just one for the three of them, number 7. Mr. Athinodoros pressed the button with the number corresponding to the employee he wanted to call, using an electric key upon his desk. Then the bell in the hallway would ring, like the chirping of an August cicada, and on the board the relevant number would stand up. Whichever of the office boys happened to be in the hall would jump up to see which number it was and then cancel it by yanking on a pull-string. Then he would run to tell the person concerned. And so Abduh's head would shoot around the door with eyes agog and shout, "Kweekly, kweekly, Mester Atinotoros he want you!"

Ugo, the Italian manager, did not have a number. Mr. Athinodoros did not call him by buzzing. Whenever he wanted to speak to him, he would stand up, open the sliding connecting door that separated their offices, and invite Ugo to join him.

If you happened to bump into Mr. Athinodoros as he was entering the office in the morning, something we all avoided, you had to say, "Good morning, Mr. Athinodoros," loud enough for him to hear—he was a little hard of hearing in one ear—but not too loud, because that would annoy him. At the same time, you had to deftly move aside for him to pass. He would reply accordingly, depending upon who had greeted him. He answered Ugo in Italian, and generally most heartily. "Buon giorno, Signor Ugo."

To one of the supervisors, or one of the older employees, he would say, "Good morning. Mr. Lefteris," or "Good morning, Mr. Alekos."

To one of the younger employees he simply said a plain "Good morning." To the office boys, all Egyptians, he said nothing at all, but simply made a slight movement with his cane as he passed. That counted less as "Good morning" than simply as "All right, I heard you." The office boys fell over themselves to be the first to rush forward and bow down low, to be the first to open the door and greet the master with *"Sabah al-kheir,"* and *"Sabah al-nur, Khawaga Atinotoros."*

Following Mr. Athinodoros in the office hierarchy came, as we have said, Signor Ugo, the office manager. He was tall, fat, swarthy, a little stooped. He moved slowly, lazily, as if he were always considering his next step. He was a good man, kind, and everyone in the office was fond of him. I often saw him joking with the senior employees. He knew how to laugh. The muscles of his face could make the necessary contractions at just the right moment to produce a pleasant expression, that outburst that we call laughter. Mr.

Athinodoros' face had no such mechanism. Nobody had ever seen him laugh, so the office staff said. But his face was not completely expressionless; in his own restrained manner he could show anger, surprise, condescension, disapproval, approbation, disappointment, satisfaction and even some pleasure. When others would have roared with laughter, Mr. Athinodoros would simply smile. His inner feelings were expressed by almost imperceptible changes in his expression that only the old-timers could recognize and interpret.

The 'news' of Mr. Athinodoros' mood swept like lightning through the office. You would suddenly see Stelios from accounts pop his head around the half-open door and say, "Mr. Athinodoros is in a good mood today," or "Oh my God! Watch out, Mr. Athinodoros is in a foul mood. Be careful."

During the year that I worked in the office I came face to face with Mr. Athinodoros only three times. The first time was a month or two after I had been hired. We met in the hallway. I was coming out of the cargo department carrying a pile of files for the accounts department.

"Mr. Lefteris, who is that young man?" Mr. Athinodoros asked my supervisor, who stood up to explain that I was the new employee. I hesitated uncertainly between the two doors. "Ah, yes," he said, as if he had suddenly remembered my case.

The second time was during one of his regular inspections of the office premises, when he suddenly appeared standing over me just as I was struggling to calculate an interminably long sum. I felt that someone was standing there, but I did not want to look up in the middle of my calculations. Without lifting my head I made a gesture which meant, "Hang on, don't interrupt me." After a while I looked up and was surprised to see Mr. Athinodoros watching me. He did not say anything, but his eyes examined my desk, and as he left he ran his finger over the desktop, gathering as he did so quite a bit of dust. He ostentatiously held his finger up to the window to see more clearly in the light. He shook his head disapprovingly as if this were a great calamity. He drew a white handkerchief from his pocket and began to wipe the dust off his finger. I wanted to laugh, it was such a comical scene. He insistently rubbed his finger as if it were covered with tar. Then he resumed his expressionless face and left the office.

The third and last time I met him it was evening. The clock on the wall showed it to be after nine. We should have finished work at eight, but we were all still at our desks. Mr. Athinodoros was closeted in his office, and, as was customary, nobody would leave before the boss. It was only in exceptional circumstances that Mr. Athinodoros gave Ugo permission to send us home before he left himself.

Mr. Alekos opened the next door down and asked Mr. Lefteris, "What's going on? Are we going to be here all night?" Lefteris, who was still busy working, did not reply, just shrugged his shoulders as if to say, "What are you asking me for? You know how things are. Why don't you let me finish my work?"

After a while the Jewish cashier came in on the pretext of wanting some document or other. "What are we going to do?" he whined. Lefteris did not reply. "What's going to happen?" the man went on in a low voice, while watching the half-open door out of the corner of his eye. "There's something I have to do, I can't stay any longer. Can I go?" He looked from Alekos to Lefteris with his cunning little eyes like tiny black marbles.

"Don't ask me," said Alekos, annoyed. "You don't expect me to give you permission, do you?"

Monsieur Abraham was not satisfied with this answer and remained there perplexed. Just then Mr. Ugo came in. Stubbornly, Monsieur Abraham continued in his efforts, "Signor Ugo, there's something I have to do. I'd like to leave. Would you allow me to go now?" And, sensing that a negative response was forthcoming, he added, "Why don't you go and ask Mr. Athinodoros if we might all leave?"

Ugo smiled mischievously. "What are you talking about? Are you crazy? You want me to get you out of this? Be patient. It's only nine o'clock. He'll be leaving soon."

"But what if he's fallen asleep?" insisted the man, who was not ready to give up his fight. Indeed, Mr. Athinodoros did occasionally fall asleep as he sat in his comfortable armchair, in which case Ugo alone could noisily enter through the connecting door on some pretext and so tactfully awaken the sleeping old man. On this particular evening, however, Ugo did not wish to take the risk and so time passed and our impatience grew.

I must say that Mr. Athinodoros' insistence upon punctuality was very one-sided, extending only to the arrival of his employees on time. The delay in leaving the office, which was a daily problem, seemed normal to him. As for overtime, the term had not yet been invented, at least not in Alexandria.

That evening I had training at the Greek Athletic Club and was very annoyed by the delay. I made a great decision: I would leave first, before Mr. Athinodoros. I gathered up my papers, picked up my sports bag, and said to my supervisor, "Mr. Lefteris, I'm off. I've got training tonight."

As he was preparing to reply, I added without waiting, "Let him fire me if he finds out . . . " Underneath, of course, I hoped that Mr. Athinodoros would not find out, but then, I thought, why should he bother with me?

Just as I was rushing past Mr. Athinodoros' office, the door suddenly opened, and the fateful meeting took place. But when I say that the door opened, I am over-simplifying matters and not adequately describing events. When Mr. Athinodoros' door opened at such a late hour, it was something like an alarm going off; a sort of sacred ceremony began. With the first creak of the hinges, one of the office boys would jump up to hold back the door, a second would leap forward to open the front door, and a third would rush to turn on the light in the stairwell while at the same time pressing the button to call the lift. In the meantime, Mr. Kleanthis, the chauffeur, would hurry down the stairs to bring the car from the nearby alleyway where it was parked. It was almost comical to watch him tumbling down the stairs two at a time, despite his age, breathlessly trying to button up his jacket, straighten his tie and adjust his cap all at the same time. At such times, Kleanthis did not leave the office, did not rush, did not descend the stairs . . . he simply vanished. It was as if he had been sucked up by some invisible power.

Mr. Athinodoros did not hurry. He savored every moment of the ritual. He had to give Kleanthis time to bring the car around to the entrance to meet him, after all. It would not be proper for him to wait on the sidewalk. When it was time, Ugo would come out into the hallway to accompany Mr. Athinodoros to the door. They would walk slowly down the hall; there was always something for them to discuss at such times. Mr. Athinodoros would pause as he walked to give emphasis to what he was saying, or he would enter one of the rooms off the hallway, on the pretext of wanting to query something. We knew it was only an excuse for him to check that all the staff were still at their posts.

And so on this particular evening, I found myself in the difficult situation of leaving at the same time as the boss. "And where are you going, Mr. Theocharis?" Mr. Athinodoros asked loudly, as if to block my escape, but also so that the others would hear what was going on. My heart was beating so loudly I thought it would jump out of my chest. I lost my tongue, but eventually found the courage to reply, "I'm going training at the club. We've got the inter-club championships on Sunday."

I said this all in a rush, like a soldier reporting to his superior officer. I took a deep breath and continued, "Will you be needing me for anything else, Mr. Athinodoros?"

He hesitated, he looked at me, and answered without anger, "No, you may go now."

The incident was discussed for many days at the office. The older members of the staff, the more prudent ones, advised me to be prepared for the end of the month, "Don't look so pleased with yourself," they said. "You never know what will happen. You don't know him that well."

As the end of the month approached, so my anxiety grew. It would not be easy to find another job. The last days of the month passed; it was good that February was short of two days. Nothing happened. That was the third and last time that Mr. Athinodoros ever concerned himself with me.

•

So, in the office hierarchy, after Mr. Athinodoros, came Signor Ugo, then Mr. Lefteris, who acted as personnel manager, then Mr. Alekos responsible for the cargo department, then Mr. Savvas the clearance broker, Monsieur Abraham the teller, followed by another twenty or so employees, all male and all Greek, with the exception of Ugo and the Abraham. At the very bottom of the hierarchy was Iordanis. After him came the three Berber office boys, Abduh, Abbas, and Aziz— 'the Three As' as we called them.

Of course, they were not Berbers but Nubians. They had those three characteristic incisions scored down both cheeks. The Europeans, however, who on the whole never attempted to understand the natives and knew nothing of their history or the origins of the various tribes, boorishly called them Berberians, Berbers, Sudanese, Nubians, or simply blacks.

Iordanis was known as just plain Iordanis, without the prefix of 'Mr.' that was added to the names of all the other European employees. Everyone spoke to him in the singular (as opposed to the plural form of the Greek that showed respect), even those younger than him. The office boys did not call him *khawaga* as they did all the other foreigners, but simply 'Iortanis.' But that was more a sign of familiarity than of lack of respect. Although Iordanis must have been almost sixty years old, everyone treated him as if he were a child.

Iordanis provided light relief in the monotonous life of the office. Although nobody gave him any serious, responsible work to do, he always managed to get things wrong.

"Hey, Iordanis, come over here. You've messed up again!" you would hear Lefteris say.

"Come here, you loafer," called Alekos. "You've missed two bills of lading off the manifest again."

"You good-for-nothing, what are these smudges? You've made a right mess of this."

Iordanis did not fit into the order and neatness of the Ath. G. Pervanidis Shipping Agency. He was careless, sloppy, clumsy. To Mr. Athinodoros, Iordanis must have represented all that he scorned, and so for me the question was, why on earth had he hired him in the first place, and why had he kept him on for so long?

Iordanis was the very opposite of Mr. Athinodoros. He was short, not fat, but chubby with a big belly. He was all rounded. His head was disproportionately large for his body, his face was round, like a circle drawn with compasses. The little hair he had stood up like the bristles on an old brush. His forehead was short, his eyebrows heavy, his nose small and round, like a meatball molded in a hurry. A little, clipped Hitler-type mustache separated his nose from his thick lips. When he smiled—which he did often and without reason—he showed his great protruding teeth, yellowed by cigarette smoke. His arms were a bit too short, and when he was standing he flapped them around as if he did not know what to do with them.

He dressed poorly, and also slovenly. His shoes were never polished, and the soles and heels were always worn. His trousers, with their wide turn-ups, vainly attempted to hold in his bulging belly. His belt, something between a scout's belt and a soldier's belt, showed beneath the short waistcoat that strained over his stomach while leaving his lower belly to hang below along with his shirttails. Whenever a button fell off it was lost forever, and only the remaining straggles of cotton bore witness to its ephemeral presence.

Iordanis' shirts were always creased, badly ironed, worn at the collar. His jacket, like all his clothes, was too tight, a sure sign that twenty years before he must have been very slim. All year round he wore the same dark gray hat with a greasy black crepe band that left a mark on his forehead. As soon as he got to the office, he would toss his hat onto the hat stand, then he would take off his jacket and hang it up and put on his black 'cashier's sleeves,' held with elastic above his elbows. He would loosen his tie, undo any buttons that were bothering him and lumber into the office with a thunderous "Ouf!" He was always out of breath. He accompanied even the simplest movement with groans and sighs.

What did he do in the office? Everything and nothing. All the other employees had specific duties, but Iordanis' job was general, undefined. Everyone gave him something to do, which as a rule he never did properly, and everyone shouted at him and complained.

The first manual calculating machines had just appeared then in Alexandria. Those complicated, heavy, and difficult-to-operate machines worked with cranks rather like a coffee grinder. Poor Iordanis tried to use one of those gadgets once, but he was so clumsy that he managed to jam the delicate, intricate gears. Rather than ask someone with more experience to help him, he began to force the crank with all his strength until he succeeded in breaking it and destroying the mechanism. He really got an earful from his colleagues as a result of that!

As a punishment, they never again gave him the 'calculator,' as they called it. And so, for the rest of his life, he was obliged to do all his calculations in his head. He hated numbers and he approached them as a long-term convict approaches forced labor and shackles. Why did they give Iordanis calculations to do when he never managed to get them right? I never could understand that.

However, Iordanis liked to write on the typewriter. He

would thump with two fingers so hard on the keys of the poor old Underwood that the whole office shook. As soon as he started to type you could hear the thud of the keys even through closed doors. They fell slowly and regularly, tak, tak, tak, like the rattle of a machine gun. The others would say, "Iordanis is at his machine gun again," and as they passed by they would tease him, saying, "Hey, nutcase, why so furious? Why are you thumping on that thing? I'll throw it out of the window," and if the colleague in question was feeling particularly witty, he would pretend to grab for the typewriter. Iordanis, without really believing this, would start shouting and pleading.

Sometimes they gave Iordanis a manifest of cargo to copy into the 'big book.' But he managed to make mistakes and smudges even with this easy task. I should say that Mr. Athinodoros did not approve of the newfangled 'Biros,' and demanded that we write in pen and ink. So Iordanis' fingers were permanently smeared and his inky finger marks were to be found everywhere.

To finish with poor Iordanis' misfortunes, I should also tell you about the torture of 'the pres,' which the staff fell back on when they had run out of trials for Iordanis. He always got in a mess with the press.

Copies of typed letters were made on the press. This was Abduh's job. It was one of the privileges of his seniority, along with the polishing of the brass. But on the pretext that Abduh was running an errand, the staff sometimes got Iordanis to have a go.

"Hey, lads, wait a bit," Iordanis would plead. "The boy will be back soon. I can't do it."

"You lazy creature, get to it," the others would urge, claiming that the copy was urgent and that Mr. Athinodoros was waiting for it.

"Ahou!" Iordanis would cry, almost in tears as he went to 'the chamber of sighs' where the press was kept.

In those days carbon paper had already appeared and you

could make copies of letters in that way. But Mr. Athinodoros treated all technical innovation with caution, and insisted that at least one copy be transferred directly into the outgoing reference book. It was a big book with thin, numbered pages made of absorbent paper. The typing of the letter was done with a special blue ink ribbon called *copiatif*. The letter went to the archives room where the press loomed. Abduh would reverently take the letter, open the book at the first blank page, and with a clean, flat brush would dampen the surface lightly with water. Then he would place the letter upon the dampened page, putting a sheet of blotting paper between, then place the closed book into the press and squeeze it with one swift, dextrous movement. That was all. The text had been printed.

The whole process looked simple but required some experience. Iordanis made an absolute mess of it. He either used too much water, in which case the excess oozed out of the press and the original letter was smudged, or he did not use enough and the copy came out faint and illegible. Despite all his suffering and troubles, Iordanis never refused to do anything he was asked.

His desk was just as untidy as he was. Messy, covered with useless piles of paper spread out all over the place. The crystal glass that topped his desk was quite a sight. Underneath it Iordanis shoved various pieces of paper and photographs. Ships, postcards, photographs of film stars, all mixed up together. Pride of place was given to a photograph of his mother, between a portrait of Valentino wearing an Arab turban from the film *Son of the Sheik*, and Greta Garbo as Queen Christina. Farther along you could see a jumble of plump, semi-naked beauties, which Iordanis had collected from the advertisements in cigarette packets. This exhibition under the glass was completed by five or six old Egyptian bank notes and the page of a calendar.

"Iordanis, what do you want those bank notes for?" Stamos, one of the new staff members, asked him one day.

"They're a memento," Iordanis replied, cutting the conversation short.

There was a strange story behind that money, which I learned by chance one evening from Iordanis himself.

•

It was a Saturday night, winter. It was raining outside. A light, monotonous, irritating rain had been falling methodically all day. Rain like that can go on for days in Alexandria. It was almost seven o'clock. Just another hour, I thought, and we can leave. Suddenly all the lights went out. We looked outside the window; the street was in darkness, the whole neighborhood was in darkness. It reminded me of the blackouts in the war. We quickly lit a candle in each of the rooms and sat down silently and patiently to wait.

The power cut found me in Iordanis' office, and as we lit the spermaceti I sat down in the chair next to his desk. I began to wonder how that last hour of the last day of the week would pass, to think about how I would meet my friends in a while at a party given by my Italian neighbor Egizio. And tomorrow, I thought, it is Sunday, a whole day without work, no office, no manifests, no ships. I looked at Iordanis absentmindedly. He had crossed his arms and was resting them on the desk. He was leaning slightly forward as if in a trance. The flickering flame of the candle reflected strangely on his face, giving him a mysterious look, almost diabolical. I thought of Cavafy's "Candles," and to myself, for no particular reason, I said, Who knows how many candles are left for Iordanis and how many for me.

It is hard to sit in the dark opposite someone with whom you have nothing to say.

Uneasily, I looked at Iordanis' desk and my eyes fell upon the corner where, under the glass, he had lined up the Egyptian bank notes one next to the other. They were old ten pound notes, soiled, almost as if mummified.

"What are those, Iordanis?" I asked him. "That's a lot of

money there. A fortune. Aren't you afraid someone will take it?"

Iordanis hesitated a little. He shuffled in his chair, moved back a bit, opened the drawer and took out his cigarettes. He smoked only Coutarellis cigarettes, because he collected the photographs of actors inside each pack.

"No. Nobody'll take it. It's old money. It's not in circulation any more." He licked his cigarette, tapped it on the glass top of his desk, as if it were to blame for his uneasiness, put it in his mouth and lit it from the flame of the candle. He inhaled deeply with obvious satisfaction, letting out the smoke all at once through his nostrils and his mouth like a harmless dragon.

"I'll tell you about them," he said, as if he had just made the great decision to let me in on a terrible secret.

I was wary of Iordanis' chatter and rushed to say that I had only asked out of curiosity and really did not want to hear any story. But Iordanis had decided not to miss the opportunity our unforeseen isolation offered and, without paying any attention to me, he began to tell his story.

•

"It was in 1918. The Great War had just ended and I had gotten a job at the Tamvakopoulos Shipping Agency—you must have heard of it," he added. "It doesn't exist anymore. I had just finished school, I had studied French, I knew some Arabic, I had learned bookkeeping—I mean, I had plenty of qualifications for those days. You see, my father, God rest his soul, wanted to give me an education. Six months went by, and everything was going wonderfully at work."

He must have seen some doubt in my eyes, because he added, "I'm not lying, don't look at the way I make mistakes these days. I don't care about the work I do now, it doesn't inspire me. And often, I must confess, I make mistakes on purpose just for the fun of it."

It was then that I realized just how monotonous and boring our life in the office would have been without Iordanis.

He leaned back again, reclining in his chair. Ignoring me, he continued. "We had a lot of work then. The port was full of ships. There were sailing ships and steamers, as well as vessels using both steam and sails. All sorts of merchandise coming into Alexandria from Greece, Constanza, England, Marseilles, Trieste. From here they loaded cotton, a great deal of cotton for England, sugar, rice, onions, linen fabric. I was in the accounts department. I was assistant to the chief accountant. We were agents not only for the big British shipping companies but for many smaller Greek traders too. They were usually owned by smaller shipowners, people who sometimes owned just the one ship and were captain of the vessel too.

"When a ship came into port, our office would usually take the captain out to dinner. That would be on the evening before the ship set sail. If it was a big ship from a large company with an English captain, Mr. Tamvakopoulos himself or the general manager would take the captain out. If it was a smaller vessel the captain would be taken out by one of the managers. If it was a trawler or a small motorship from Greece, then one of the older members of the staff would look after the captain.

"One evening we were to take out a captain from Andros who was owner of a small ship under five hundred tons.

"The chief accountant asked, 'Who's going to take Captain Manolis out for dinner?' His expression clearly showed that he had no intention of dealing with such an insignificant captain. It was Saturday evening. Nobody seemed prepared to volunteer.

"'Stamatis will do it,' someone said.

"'No, I can't,' Stamatis said stubbornly.

"'Well, let Stergios do it then.' But Stergios refused too.

"'Is this a game we're playing?' asked the manager, annoyed, and realizing that nobody was interested in accepting the charge, he said, looking in my direction, 'Iordanis will take him out.'"

•

At this stage, Iordanis took a deep breath and drew deeply on his cigarette before going on. "Imagine my position. I was just twenty years old and the agency was going to entrust me to take out a real shipowner.

"Perhaps Captain Manolis only had the *Platytera*, but he was an old sea-dog who had battled with the seas since childhood, and to buy that old Scottish hull he had sold—so they said—three sailing vessels that he had owned before with his brothers.

"I felt suddenly as if I had grown up. As if I were taller. I willingly accepted the job and went home to get ready. I put on my dark, pinstriped suit, white shirt with starched collar, my good tie. I mean, I was dressed to kill!"

Just then he noticed his belly sticking out of the tight waist-coat, and said, "Well, it's over thirty years ago. Don't look at me now."

He continued. "I knew from the other employees what went on when they took captains out. The office provided you with Mr. Tamvakopoulos' car, a smart black Renault, and its driver, Anestis, a weedy man from Corfu with enormous mustaches. You would go to the port, pick up the captain from his ship, and drive to one of the Greek restaurants on the coast road.

"So, as I was saying, I got all dressed up. Put brilliantine on my hair—I had plenty of hair in those days—put on my homburg hat. I stuffed the two pounds that the cashier had given me to cover expenses deep into my pocket and set off. My heart was all aflutter.

"When Anestis opened the car door for me and I enthroned myself upon the back seat, I felt like the khedive on his way to a ceremony. I had never been in a car before. I'd only been in a landau carriage a couple of times. Automobiles were rare in those days. We used to walk almost everywhere.

"Anyway, to cut a long story short, we picked up Captain Manolis, a bowlegged, slightly built, middle-aged islander with huge hands like spades, which were rough from salt water and tar—when he shook your hand it was like being scratched by sandpaper. He was wearing a seaman's cap. He got into the car and we set off for the Corniche. We reached Kallithea, a small restaurant that served Greek *mezze*, wine, *zibib,* and beer. As we ate, our glasses were filled and refilled. 'Cheers, Captain Manolis,' we went, and 'To your very good health, young man.' And so the evening passed.

"I had only ever drunk beer once before, at my cousin Penelope's wedding. I generally only drank lemonade. But whenever I tried to stop, the captain would shout 'To your health' in his thunderous voice as if he were giving orders to his boatswain. And our glasses would be filled again until the empty beer bottles and the empty *zibib* carafes covered the table in columns like soldiers on parade. I was a bit woozy. But I felt good and very talkative. The only thing that was worrying me was whether the two pounds would be enough to cover the bill. I didn't want to look foolish.

"Of course, two pounds was a lot of money in those days. My salary then was five pounds. The two pounds was more than enough and there was plenty left to leave a good *baksheesh* for the waiters who bowed to us when I told them to keep the change.

"The world was at my feet. In my imagination I had already come a long way. I saw myself climbing the ladder at work; I'd become a supervisor, and, why not, even manager and one day a shipowner. My dreams and ambitions were lightly floating in the froth of the beer.

"Captain Manolis, who had drunk both beer and *zibib,* was blind drunk. He was rambling about the ship that he had paid for, about his daughter Crystallo who he was ready to marry off. After leaving Alexandria, he'd be heading for Bengazi and from there to Piraeus.

"We stood up. Then I realized that I was very drunk.

Everything was spinning and I said to myself, Holy Virgin, I'm done for. I'm bound to fall over. But as soon as we left the restaurant, the cool breeze restored my senses some. The two of us staggered toward the car and a little later we parted on the companionway of the ship, after Captain Manolis had sent a cabin boy to bring me a gift of two pots of honey, a jar of olives, and some mastic from Chios. To remember him by, he said.

"Anestis took me home. I must have been really drunk because my mother, who was waiting up for me, started shouting when she saw me, 'What time do you call this? Just look at the state of you. You're drunk!'

"I don't remember anything else, I just fell straight into bed and I couldn't get up in the morning. It was Sunday, but we worked a half-day on Sundays then. I only just made it in to the office as the others were getting ready to leave.

"'What happened to you, lad?' Mr. Iosif asked me. I blushed as I explained that I had been out late the night before with the captain and that I wasn't used to beer and it had upset me a bit. Apart from that, I was proud, I had carried out my duty to the full.

"'Well done, lad,' said Mr. Iosif. 'Good show.'

"I handed in the bill from the restaurant and everything went back to normal.

"For me, of course, something had changed, because I felt as if I had been promoted, I had become important. I had been entrusted with a serious mission and I expected it to be repeated sometime. I'd been in an automobile, something as significant in those days as getting on an airplane is now."

Suddenly, Iordanis paused. "Have you ever been on an airplane?"

I admitted that I had only ever been in a car twice, a taxi.

"You see," he said, obviously satisfied. "Imagine what it was like then, in 1918."

I was speechless. Before me a different Iordanis was revealed. A transformed Iordanis. A stranger to me. Iordanis with ambitions, dreams, unlike the Iordanis I knew who clumsily thumped the keys of the poor old typewriter.

Time passed, but the lights did not come back on. It was eight o'clock and I could hear my colleagues one by one going down the hallway as they left. Mr. Athinodoros had allowed us to leave a few minutes earlier because of the power cut. But how could I leave? I was consumed by curiosity to hear the rest of the story.

"Go on, Iordanis," I said. "Finish the story so we can leave too."

"Yes," he said, as if coming round, "I'll finish it."

"For a month or so, everything was fine. They brought me a new typewriter, an Underwood, and we began to write some correspondence on that, while the rest we still wrote in pen and ink. I even suggested that we wrote the bills of lading on the typewriter. That was considered a revolutionary idea.

"One day, a letter arrived from Captain Manolis. Someone else must have written it for him, because he was illiterate himself. It was addressed to Mr. Iosif, the supervisor of the accounts department, and among other things, he asked why the statement of accounts for his voyage had not been credited with the 50 pounds he had given—so he said—to Mr. Iordanis Trandalidis. He explained that as he was to go to Piraeus after Bengazi, during the dinner, which we had been kind enough to provide, he had given the employee of the agency the sum of 50 pounds to be credited to his account.

"'Iordanis,' Mr. Iosif said to me with a severe expression, 'Why didn't you say anything about the money? We've been put in a very awkward position.'

"The blood rushed to my head. My mind was blurred. My eyes went dark and I stuttered, 'But what money, Mr. Iosif? When . . . where . . . from whom?'

"'Come on, lad, what are you talking about? The letter's clear enough. Come and read it for yourself.'

"How was I supposed to read it? My hands were trembling, the lines were swimming before me, I couldn't see a thing.

"'But I swear, I didn't take any money . . . '

"'Oh come on now . . . that's not possible,' said Mr. Iosif, and he became even sterner. Soon the letter came into the hands of Mr. Tamvakopoulos. The issue had taken on dimensions. Fifty pounds was no small matter. To me it was an exorbitant amount. Ten months' salary.

"I thought I'd go crazy. I was quite aware of the seriousness of the matter. I was in a panic. I tried to control my thoughts, to gather the fleeting images that mixed themselves up in my brain. They jostled with each other and I couldn't put them into any sort of order. I said to myself, Calm down, Iordanis, and I tried to re-enact what had happened that night, minute by minute. I could remember everything, despite my wooziness after the last few glasses of beer, but nowhere could I remember receiving any money. The only money I could recall was the bank notes I used to pay the bill. I racked my brains. Nothing. A complete blank."

•

Reliving the events filled Iordanis with anguish. He sighed, he puffed like a trapped seal, his face was sweating, and he kept wiping it with the black sleeve-coverings. He stubbed out a cigarette and immediately lit up another. He went on. "To cut a long story short, after a while Mr. Iosif came out of the boss's office and said to me in a harsh voice, 'Have you remembered anything?'

"'But what am I supposed to remember? Are you serious? I don't know anything, I swear.'

"He ordered me to follow him into Mr. Tamvakopoulos' office. My heart was pounding, I was sweating, my legs had turned to jelly. How did I get into this mess, I thought? I'm done for.

"I pinched myself just to check that I wasn't dreaming, but unfortunately I was awake. There I was in the boss's office.

Apart from Mr. Tamvakopoulos, the manager, the personnel manager, and two or three other supervisors were standing there too, with their arms folded across their chests.

"They really interrogated me. Interrogation? More like the Inquisition. I stuck to my story. I couldn't remember receiving any money, not even any small change. One of them called me a 'thieving rascal,' another called me a 'scoundrel.' They all called me a villain. When they had run out of abuse, they left me standing there in a corner like a schoolboy being punished while they gathered round in a circle to deliberate. They spoke quietly, but loud enough for me to hear. 'Let's call the police.'

"'No,' Mr. Tamvakopoulos said, 'we'll call the *kavassis* from the consulate to take him straight to the judge.'

"I should explain," said Iordanis, "that in those days the Mixed Courts, the Tribunaux Mixtes, had not yet been abolished. The Egyptian courts had no jurisdiction over foreign subjects, whatever crime they had committed. Even a felony. The responsible body was the Mixed Court, which was made up of European judges—English, French, Italians, Greeks.

"They talked and talked . . . I don't know if they really meant what they said or whether they were whispering like that just to frighten me into confessing. But what could I confess? If they had stood me before the gallows they couldn't have gotten a confession out of me for something which I felt I had not done.

"Mr. Iosif spoke last. He spoke more quietly than the others. I only heard what he said because he spoke very slowly and because all the others had fallen silent and his words echoed in the silence of the office.

"'Just a moment, gentlemen. Something is amiss here. The boy denies it insistently. He's a good lad. He's been with us for almost a year and he's been a model employee. He's from a good family. He's the son of Trandalidis. I suggest we send a telegram to the agent in Piraeus and ask Captain Manolis for clarification. We can't lop off his head without investigating the matter in depth. And anyway, even if things are as they seem, let's give him some time for soul searching, to think, to find the money.'

"Nobody agreed with Mr. Iosif's suggestion, but he was the most senior member of staff, and the oldest, and his opinion carried weight. They composed the telegram and sent it off. It took two weeks for an answer to arrive, because, it seems, Captain Manolis was away.

"I was literally out of my mind. Almost crazy. So was my mother, who searched through the pockets of the suit I had worn that night over and over again.

"'Why are you going through them again, Mama? I've told you, I don't recall taking any money,' I cried, frustrated. My mother had searched through all my clothes, all my trousers, all my jackets, all my waistcoats. I even searched the car with old Anestis, the chauffeur, in case there was anything under the seats.

"My life was hell. I went to the office but I was ashamed to look my colleagues in the face. I thought they were all talking about me. Even so, I still hoped that when the reply came from the captain it would say that there had been a mistake, that the money was in his cabin, that he had never given it to me.

"But the telegram when it came—written in Franco-Levantine Greek—was laconic but unambiguous: 'In response to your telegram I confirm that the sum of 50 Egyptian pounds was given to your employee Mr. Iordanis.'

"'What do you have to say for yourself?' Mr. Iosif asked me. And he showed me the text.

"I had made my decision. I declared for the last time, 'I didn't take the money.' And without waiting for them to fire me or haul me off to the court, I left the office.

"It nearly killed my mother. My father had died just a year before. I hid in the house and for two years I didn't dare to even think of going out to look for work.

"When I went out occasionally for an evening, to try to forget, to walk a bit as far as the Corniche, I felt as if everyone was talking about me, pointing at me in the street. On Sundays when we went to Evangelismos for the service, I felt that all eyes were suspiciously upon me. I imagined what they were whispering to each other as I passed. What they would say when they got home: 'That's Trandalidis' son. His father was a good man, but he's a good-for-nothing. He stole 50 pounds from Tamvakopoulos.'

"After two years, I realized that my mother couldn't make ends meet, that the little money she had from the sale of my father's shop had been used up. I had to get a job on an *ezba* in Zagazig. I kept the books for an Egyptian cotton producer, Suliman Pasha. I kept an eye on the supervisors, paid the wages. My Uncle Minas got me the job, God rest his soul. I stayed there for thirty whole years, until the day the pasha died.

"I lived a quiet life in Zagazig. Hidden, enclosed within myself among the fellahin who toiled to produce the 'white gold.' When I arrived, I never thought I'd be there for so long. I thought I'd stay a while until the truth came out. I was young and inexperienced and I believed that because I was innocent the truth would shine out of its own accord. The day would come when, as if by magic, like in fairy tales, I would be vindicated and everyone would say, Iordanis was right all along.

"It's all just an adventure, I told myself, the truth will come out, or I'll go crazy.

"The days passed, the years passed, and nothing happened, nothing new. The pasha, the owner of the *ezba*, was a good man. He trusted me, and that's why I stayed for so long. The work was hard but not complicated. There was no opportunity for me to make mistakes because everyone else knew so much less than I did. Nobody knew how to read. Only a few knew how to count. The pasha was illiterate too, but he knew how to count. He knew what was in his best interest, and he knew that I protected his interests. Things ran like clockwork, almost on their own. Night followed day and then the sun came up again. At first light the fellahin set to work and at nightfall we all went to sleep. We ate something in between, of course.

"The Nile rose and fell regularly. Swelled and overflowed its banks. The fields were flooded. Then as if by habit the waters receded, leaving behind the thick mud that the river had brought from the distant mountains of Ethiopia and Sudan. It is to that mud that the Nile Valley owes its fertility, that blessed mud. Over and over again for thousands and thousands of years.

"The fellahin had been molded out of that mud, they had become one with it. They splashed around in it all day. Their huts were built of it. Their children made dolls out of it. Mud, sweat under the blazing sun, and a continual song sung in chorus, always monotonous, never sad. There I felt how man can overcome the mud, how he can stand above it with hope, without sinking.

"Fine, Iordanis, you say, but let's move on. Let's finish with this story. What happened after that?"

But Iordanis was in no mood to shorten his tale now that he had found someone to listen. He continued. "I followed the ways of the fellah, the ways of the Nile. I moved just as the ox trudged around and around the well—the *noria*—that gave us water. The only difference was that the ox was blinkered so that he would not get dizzy. My eyes were wide open and I could see the horizon all around marked out by the date palms, willowy, towering, proudly holding up their bodies high above the cotton plantation.

"I didn't dare return to Alexandria. I was ashamed of an offense that I had not committed. My poor mother, God bless her, wrote to me every week and came to see me two or three times a year: Christmas, Easter, and sometimes during the feast of Bairam. I couldn't forget the missing 50 pounds; it tortured me during the day and haunted my nights.

"Tamvakopoulos didn't carry out his threat to take me to

Athinodoros and Iordanis **121**

court, but the fear stayed with me for many years. What really bothered me, even though the years passed, was finding a solution to the mystery of that incredible story. But what could I do? I couldn't do anything more than go over and over the events of that fateful evening moment by moment. I made up different scenarios in my mind, each more fantastic than the other. The predominant scenario was that my colleagues at the office had been jealous of me and had used Captain Manolis to get rid of me. At other times I reflected that perhaps—you know how seamen are—the captain had spent the money on women in some port. But none of these ideas satisfied me. I thought them silly, farfetched, and I kept coming back to face that enormous unsolved question once more alone.

"When the pasha died and his estate was inherited by his nephews, I left Zagazig. I returned to Alexandria. During the thirty years that I had spent with the fellahin, I had only visited Alexandria twice, for a few days—the first time when I was ill with a gastric infection and the second when I had some teeth out.

"I couldn't look for work because I didn't dare show myself too much in the city. I imagined that despite the years that had passed, someone would recognize me. When I went out to do some shopping for my mother, I felt as if people were looking at me curiously and I thought, Ah! he knows me. He must be saying to himself, there's Iordanis, the thief. He's back.

"But I was not out of work for long, because my mother's cousin, Mr. Athinodoros, returned from England."

Iordanis saw my questioning look, and added, "Yes, I'm related to Mr. Athinodoros. He and my mother are second or third cousins. I don't mention it much at work because I don't want the others to be jealous. He's a good man, Athinodoros, he took me into the office at once.

"The question of the fifty pounds remained a mystery until two years ago."

He stopped for a while, swallowed hard, smiled in an embarrassed way and went on. "Two years ago, just before Easter, I was helping my mother to clean the house—she's almost eighty, but she manages just fine. She got me to tidy up the bookcase. I took down all the books, hundreds of books. They were all my father's—he was a bookseller and he adored books. As I was dusting them one by one, I came across a small book of poems. I don't remember who they were by. I don't read poetry—never have. Whenever I tried I never managed to get past the first few lines. But when I came to dust this little book, I don't know what happened, but some force pushed me to open it, to browse through its pages. And as I opened it, what did I see? Five ten pound notes.

"I was flabbergasted. I felt an emptiness inside, as if my body was suddenly hollow, as if my heart had stopped beating. 'Holy Virgin!' I shouted. 'It's Captain Manolis' money!' My heart began to beat again, strong, fast, and irregular—it kicked. Then it was as if I had woken up from a thirty-year-long dream. I remembered everything.

"That night at the tavern, I had taken the book of poetry along. What for? I wanted to show that I was literate. Show who? Captain Manolis . . . who couldn't read a word himself. When we were ready to leave, Captain Manolis went to pay the bill. Of course, I wouldn't let him. He had taken out his wallet and he was insisting, but I told him that I had my orders from the office and that I was to pay. It was then, it seems, that he gave me the fifty pounds that he had on him to be credited to the account of the ship, as he was leaving the next day and wouldn't be needing them. Woozy as I was, drunk for the first time in my life, I put the money inside the book. I couldn't remember that for thirty years.

"I felt a mixture of satisfaction and guilt. At last the mystery had been solved, but the facts were against me. Captain Manolis had been right; I had taken the money. I rushed to tell my mother. She was at a loss for words, as if she had been struck by a thunderbolt. Before she had recovered, she fell on her knees in front of the icons, crossed herself and gave thanks to Saint Fanourios for performing this miracle, for revealing the truth and my innocence. I paused for a while and contemplated. I thought it had taken the saint a very long time to decide to perform his miracle, but I said better late than never!

"Then I felt a crazy need to rush out and see all those people who I had avoided over the past thirty years, to tell them that the mystery had been solved, to show them the money, the old bank notes. I rushed to Tamvakopoulos' office. Everything seemed as if just a few days had passed since I was last there. I knew that Tamvakopoulos had died, the company had been sold, but I thought, I'm bound to find someone. But none of the old employees were there. Some had died, others had moved on. Only Salem, the youngest in the office in those days, was still there. He recognized me.

"'Khawaga Iortanis, how are you? Where have you been?' He grasped both my hands warmly, obviously moved to see me. I thought at least I could tell Salem my story. I showed him the money, feeling sure that he knew all about it. Immediately I realized that the poor man had no idea what I was talking about and he started to look at me strangely as if I were unbalanced.

"I left the office and began to run through the streets looking for someone who would know me, who would know what had happened, so that I could tell him how things had turned out. I couldn't find anybody I knew anywhere. Some had died, others had left. But at the Customs House, I found Nikos, who had been assistant to our clearance broker. He was surprised when he saw me; he thought I had died. Even he knew nothing of my misfortune and he listened to me confused, as if he thought I was mad. Disappointed, I went home. I said to myself, never mind, tomorrow I'll tell my colleagues at the office.

"The next day I began with Mr. Grigoris. He had no idea.

'Iordanis, what money are you talking about? Let me get on with my work, will you?'

"Frustrated, I rushed to Mr. Alekos. Same thing. Nobody knew anything about it. They hadn't heard about my misfortune. Eventually, Grigoris said, 'Iordanis has finally gone completely nuts. Let me have a look at that money, you. Hey, it's useless. You can't use these any more. They're from the khedive's times. Where on earth did you find them?'

"I knocked on Mr. Athinodoros' door—something I had never done before. But at that moment I found the courage to do absolutely anything. I showed him the bank notes. I told him the story. He knew all about it; my mother had told him. He listened to me carefully. He looked at me and said almost kindly, 'Iordanis, I know you are honest.'

"I burst into tears. I cried like a child. I had spent all my life bearing the burden of an offense I had not committed. I had hidden, thinking that everyone was talking about me, when in fact nobody knew or cared what had happened. At any rate, a weight was lifted from me, that weight that had been crushing down upon me for so long."

•

It was as if there had been a conspiracy, as if fate had taken pity on Iordanis and, with the power cut, had obliged me to sit and listen to his story. As soon as he had finished, the lights came back on.

We were blinded by the sudden light. We squinted in the glare. We got up. Iordanis spat on two fingers and pinched the flame of the candle to extinguish it.

"Let's go, Iordanis," I said. "The others have left already. Come on, before Abduh locks us in."

Iordanis seemed moved. Slowly, he took off the black sleeve-coverings and rubbed his arms where the elastic had pinched. Then he put on his homburg hat, and looked at the desktop that held the old bank notes.

"Damned money," he murmured. "You ruined my life."

And then, out loud, he said to me, "Who knows, if it hadn't been for those infernal bits of paper, I might have done something significant with my life. I might have been the manager of a shipping company. I might even have been a shipowner. I'd pass by and people would say, 'That's Mr. Iordanis Trandalidis. He owns five ships.'"

We had gone down the stairs and were out on the street. I did not know what to say. Iordanis' story had upset me. Just then, Mr. Athinodoros' car drew up and Kleanthis, as he opened the rear door, signaled to us that the boss was coming out behind us. We moved aside for Mr. Athinodoros to pass, while Iordanis, with hat in hand, bade him farewell with a respectful gesture. Then he turned to me, put his hat on, shook his head and said, "Never mind, that's life. See you on Monday then, God willing."

Amm Ahmad, Father and Son

Amm Ahmad was the janitor in the *okella* where we lived. To be more precise, I should say, he was the *bawwab*— that's what we called the janitors in Egypt. A tall, gangly Nubian of indeterminate age. If you had said he was eighty, you might have been doing him an injustice; perhaps he was just a wizened sixty-year-old.

He was literally skin and bone. His shrunken skin was the color of rust and stuck to his bones, seeming almost to hold them together. He reminded me of a pharaonic mummy. When I first saw the mummy of Ramses II in the Cairo Museum, I thought, "Hey! He's the spitting image of Amm Ahmad . . . "

Amm Ahmad used to take us to school and pick us up again in the afternoons when my brother and I were in the lower classes of junior school. It was just one of the umpteen duties of a *bawwab*. From dawn till dusk he ran errands. He was always either unclogging the drains for the Maltese on the second floor, taking a tray of cookies to the baker's for Kyria Magdalene, or carrying shopping for the teacher, an old maid who lived on the ground floor.

Amm Ahmad walked with a limp, which made him seem to hop along, but he moved with an agility that would have made any young lad jealous. He strode along so fast that we had trouble keeping up with him. He would hold tightly onto our hands to make sure we did not slip away, his bony fingers gripping like pincers. When we used to complain about the speed at which he hauled us along, Amm Ahmad would try to turn things into a game, making train noises as he went—chuff, chuff, chuff—so he could drag us along with less resistance. It was not so much his pace that bothered me—I could not keep up with his stride, so I had to trot alongside him in any case—but the fact that the *bawwab* would not let me stop to gaze at the shops that so enchanted me.

At Christmas in particular, the shop windows were a sheer joy: Christmas trees loaded down with decorations, manger scenes with tiny, colorful statuettes, Father Christmas, reindeer, angels, and artificial snow. But apart from all that, the shop windows filled up with a wonderful array of toys. Not during the war, of course—such things disappeared from the shops then. But in our house, even when things were in short supply and the bombing was heavy, we still had Christmas presents and Father Christmas still arrived with startling punctuality.

Much later I learned that, for months beforehand, my father had sat up at night making wooden toys for us himself. Soldiers, airplanes, tanks, guns—as if the real ones were not enough. Why did my father, a quiet, peace-loving man, make us such military toys, I wonder? But we liked them, and looked forward with great enthusiasm to Christmas morning, when we could open our presents.

•

But let us get back to Amm Ahmad . . . Eventually, our grumbling mixed up with train noises, we would reach the entrance to our *okella*, puffing and out of breath. When we got to the *bawwaba*, Amm Ahmad would let go his grip and my brother and I would both rush up the marble staircase, bounding up the steps two at a time, to see who could get to the top and ring the doorbell first.

Having completed his task, Amm Ahmad would disappear into his little room in the *bawwaba*. This room confused me—it was, to me, a mysterious place, something like Ali Baba's cave. I had never been inside Amm Ahmad's 'den,' but it had to be small, quite tiny in fact. How much space could there *be* under the staircase? And yet it seemed like the magic box at the circus as, apart from the old *bawwab* himself, his wife and a whole brood of children piled out of the *bawwaba*. How did they all fit in there? How did they cook? How did they sleep? I had no idea.

In accordance with his rights under Islamic law, Amm Ahmad had three wives. "I could have had more," I heard him say once, when talking to the Shami upholsterer. "The Prophet—in his great wisdom—allows me to have up to four wives provided, of course, that I care for them all. But I, praise be to the Almighty, have only three, and I'm not complaining. That's enough for me."

I had only seen the youngest of Amm Ahmad's wives. Her name was Noura—or Fotini, in Greek, which means 'luminous.' She was the wife who lived with him in the *bawwaba*. She was petite, and you could tell from her eyes that she was young and pretty, as the eyes were the only part of her that was visible behind the black *milaya* and veil that she wore. The *bawwab*'s other wives lived in outlying suburbs, where he went to visit them from time to time. I heard that the oldest wife, who he had been married to for some forty years, lived in Karmuz, while the second, whom he had married at the end of the Great War, lived in Anfushi. These were poor Arab quarters where no European ventured.

Noura must have been considered very lucky. She was poor, and Amm Ahmad had married her during the last war. She had found a husband during those difficult years, a husband with a good, steady job. The position of *bawwab* was considered by poor Egyptians to be a reliable, stable job. You did not need to be educated, and it was permanent, almost like being a civil servant. The *bawwab* was a person you could trust; he knew everyone's secrets. He knew who went in and out of the *okella*. He rarely lost his job; when a *bawwab* got a position, it was for life, and the *bawwaba* was often inherited by his eldest son.

How many children did Amm Ahmad have? Only he could answer that question for sure. Even Noura, when my mother asked her once, was confused, and said, "Do you mean, all together?"

"Why, yes, dear. All of them—yours as well as his other children."

"I don't know," she replied shyly, "I don't ask him such things." And then, as if she had given it some thought, she went on, "I suppose there must be about fifteen. There are my four, anyway, two boys and two girls."

We rarely saw Noura and her children. How did they spend their time? How did they live packed into that tiny room? Questions that remained unanswered. Whenever there was a feast, the Great or the Small Bairam, or *Shamm al-Nesim*, then Amm Ahmad would appear dressed in his best white *gallabiya*, with Noura wrapped in her black *milaya* from head to toe, and their four children, barefoot, runny-nosed, gummy-eyed, each holding a colorful sugar doll—an *arusa*.

On those holidays all the Egyptians took to the streets. They set out from the distant, poor suburbs, spreading out through the European districts, until they reached the coast, the public gardens, and the grand squares. They came out like swarms of ants, causing such a crowded crush that it was difficult to even walk in the streets. It was like a huge human tide that slowly spread out all over the city through-out the day, only subsiding as the sun went down, and dis-appearing with the last call of the muezzin to evening prayer.

Apart from the four small children that Amm Ahmad had with Noura, one of the children by his second wife lived with them. His name was Badri. He was a well-built, dark boy, around my age. I remember Badri as being short, some-what squarish, with a short neck, intelligent eyes, and a goodhearted smile showing sparkling white teeth. I used to play with Badri when I was at junior school. He had never been to school himself and only just knew how to read a few lines of the Quran, which an old sheikh had taught him.

"The Good Book says it all; all the wisdom of the world is held within," Sheikh Ramadan used to say.

When Badri was ten years old, his father sent him to Zagazig, to a cotton plantation where an uncle of his worked. He stayed there with the fellahin for five or six years, returning to Alexandria at the beginning of the 1950s to settle down once more in the *bawwaba* with Amm Ahmad's family, helping out, sharing the work with his father.

The 1950s were troubled years in the history of modern Egypt. Nationalism was on the rise. You could feel that the Egyptians were trying to shake off not only foreign oppression, but also that of the local oligarchy. In 1951 there were mass demonstrations in the streets. Egypt denounced the treaty of 1936, which imposed the presence of British troops on the Suez Canal. Their final withdrawal had been arranged for 1956. Suddenly, in 1952, there was a *coup d'état*, and Farouk was deposed.

I remember that it was a hot summer's day. Farouk, corrupt and incompetent, went into exile with his family. He gathered up all that he could, boarded his luxury yacht *Mahrusa* and left for Italy. There was great joy and celebration. The locals took to the streets. Many did not really understand what was going on, while the old men shook their heads: what was the world coming to? In the cafés, they talked in hushed tones about developments, sipping the traditional steaming hot tea and smoking their *shisha* with great relish. New words and new names, heard for the first time, spread across the Great City: revolution, revolutionary council, democracy, General Naguib, Gamal Abd al-Nasser, Abd al-Hakim Amer, Anwar Sadat . . .

Badri was beside himself. He was all puffed up with pride.

"You'll see," he said. "Things'll be fine. We'll throw the 'Yehudis,' the Zionists, out of Palestine, they'll leave Arab soil. And the foreigners must leave our country too. This land is ours."

Of course, Badri allowed for some exceptions, and he reassured us that we did not have to leave, just as the other good folk who lived in our three-story *okella* did not have to go either. He also made an exception for old Thanasis, the tobacconist who used to give him sweets when he was small, and who now let him flick through the magazines and newspapers in his shop.

The little *bawwab* said that soon he would be off to join the army, to fight the hated Jews. He would learn to read and write, and might even become an officer. He was so enthusiastic, almost drunk with his own words, waving his arms about as he spoke . . . So many dreams long betrayed, so many desires never fulfilled, so many smothered hopes. Link after link in a long chain, generation after generation, raked up passions from the depths of time.

Another two years went by. In 1954 Naguib stood down and his place was taken by the true leader of the revolution, Gamal Abd al-Nasser, who was to stamp his personality upon a whole era.

•

And yet another two years passed—it was July 1956.

"Have you heard?" said Pavlos. "Nasser is coming to Alexandria tomorrow. He's going to speak in Muhammad Ali Square."

My friend Pavlos was from a leftist family. Politically savvy, he was following developments closely.

"We'll go and hear him speak," he went on, "and we'll take Amm Ahmad's son along with us."

It was mid-summer. A hot wind, like a *khamsin*, had just died down, leaving the city full of the hot breath of the desert. The date trees were heavy with ripe fruit. Clusters of dates hung like the heavy udders of cows waiting to be milked. The slightest breeze bent the tree trunks, causing the treetops to nudge conspiratorially against each other, as if exchanging secret messages of what was to come. The sweet

scent of *full* and jasmine was so strong, it seemed to be trying to drive people crazy. And yet the people paid no attention. They seemed not to notice. They bent insistently over their radio sets, and those who could read gobbled up the newspapers hungrily. They were trying to grasp what was going on. They took on serious expressions, which ill-suited their cheerful Egyptian faces, and discussed events in whispers.

"It's already been four years since the revolution," said Pavlos, "and the nation is still waiting to see better days. The people are still hungry."

It was true. Of course, great efforts had been made, but as Ismail said, "Things like that don't change overnight. It takes time and patience. We don't want to lose what little we have."

The foreigners were wary of the revolution.

"If Nasser succeeds, other countries under foreign rule will follow his example. There'll be uprising everywhere." Pavlos said this with an intense expression on his face, in a loud voice, almost as if he were giving a speech. I looked to see if perhaps he was talking to other people around us, but we were alone.

"You're right, Pavlo," I said, "but we could get into trouble going to the meeting. Remember last time, at the demonstration for Algerian independence? When the *shawish* showed up, you ran off and I took a beating."

"Don't talk rubbish. Things have changed since then. Haven't you noticed?" He said this with such disarming certainty, as if he were amazed by my naiveté.

Nasser wanted to build a great dam in Aswan. This *Sadd al-Aali* had become an obsession with him. He wished to tame the waters of the Nile that gushed out into the sea. If a giant dam could be built, the flow could be controlled, and, the experts said, vast expanses of desert could be irrigated and the people would never go hungry again.

But the coffers were empty and Egypt wanted help from the West. They asked the World Bank to finance this 'Great

Work.' It seems that, at first, America and Britain were fairly positive about it, but as time passed they began to drag their feet. The nation waited with bated breath. Nasser's speech in Alexandria would be, they said, of the utmost significance. Countless people from all over the country set out to hear the *rais*, the leader, speak—young, old, and children alike, but very few women, as on such occasions they generally stayed at home.

They came by train, by bus, by tram, in carts, on donkeys, and on foot. From early in the morning, they began to gather at the stations, parks, and squares, outside the mosques and the cafés, and in the afternoon they began to move toward the great square. They approached like a gathering swarm of locusts: ten became a hundred, a hundred became a thousand and grew into a myriad.

When we reached the square, it was packed with Egyptians. As far as the eye could see, nothing but the white turbans worn by those in *gallabiyas*, the occasional red tarboosh and black tassel worn by those who dressed in the European fashion, numerous *taqiyas*—small white or darkgray skullcaps—and many bare, dark heads too, defying the savage sun. There was not a European to be seen; they were nervous, they had stayed at home, talking once again of times gone by, of uprising and the terrible deeds of the locals that made your hair stand on end. All these stories came suddenly to mind and I wondered, "Will there be trouble again?"

As the hour approached for the arrival of the president, so the sea of bodies swelled, and from the crowd came a roar, like the angry tide. The mass could no longer be contained within the boundaries of the vast stone square, and began to overflow into the side streets, flooding the alleys and pouring outward toward the coast. Then a whisper started up that became louder and louder until it was a deafening hum: "It's him, he's here, he's here . . . "

What an uproar! From where we were standing I could see

Nasser, a tall figure standing on a balcony, with outspread arms, greeting the crowd. Everyone was jumping up and down. Carried away by the atmosphere, Pavlos and Badri joined in. The villagers, the *sa'idi*s, jumped up and down too, wielding their staffs above their heads like swords.

And then the moment came: through the tinny megaphones, the voice of the leader was heard; calm, serene, firm. All at once, the crowd fell silent, hanging on Nasser's every word. Not a sound. We stood stock still, as if petrified, as if in that huge square the impassioned revolutionary and the bronze horseman, seemingly powerless on his high pedestal, faced each other alone, like ancient gladiators.

Pavlos had commented earlier that the mounted statue of Muhammad Ali—the founder of the dynasty that Nasser had abolished—should be pulled down. "It's a symbol of oppression. It's got to go," he said.

I said nothing, but I thought, "It would be a great shame if such a beautiful sculpture were to be lost." Fortunately, the statue of the mounted pasha did survive.

As the speech went on, so Nasser's tone rose. Now, he irately explained to the people the refusal of the foreigners to finance the building of the great dam at Aswan. "We asked for the money to build the *Sadd al-Aali*, but Mr. Black, president of the World Bank, showed that he has a soul as black as his name. They denied us the money. They denied well-being to the Egyptian people. But we will build the Great Work. Our homeland will continue on the road toward its destiny."

He paused, and added in a strong voice, stressing each and every word: "I hereby declare the nationalization of the Suez Canal. The canal belongs to us, and the income from the tolls charged for passage through it will build our dam."

The square was frozen. The audience realized that they were experiencing a historic moment. There was a pause that seemed to last forever, as if everything were hanging in the air. And then the crowd began to cheer, chanting over and over again: "Gamal, Gamal, Gamal . . . " Gamal Abd al-Nasser had dared to stand up to the superpowers of Britain and France.

The president spoke for a while longer, but he could not be heard above the din of the celebrations. It was an outburst of suppressed pride that had been simmering for years in this great granite pot. Nasser left. Night fell, but the square was still crowded. The people had been taken over by a sacred passion; nobody wanted to leave and the pulsating square refused to empty.

How long did the celebrations last? I cannot remember. It seemed that time had stopped. At some point, the square was surrounded by firemen with water hoses who doused the crowd. That calmed everyone down. Soaked to the skin, we set off for home. Elated, Pavlos was gesticulating wildly, he was so carried away by his enthusiasm. So was Badri, who could not contain his joy and said he was going to sign up for the forces immediately.

But things became difficult over the next few months as the French and British decided on military intervention in a vain attempt to maintain control of the canal. The Israelis took advantage of the situation and attacked too, claiming that Nasser refused to allow their ships through the canal. Israel advanced rapidly and occupied Sinai. In just one hundred hours they had reached the Suez Canal.

Despite the fact that the media did not reveal the true extent of the situation and spoke of the enemy's "heavy losses," the wind went out of the Egyptians' sails. But not for long, because soon, under heavy international pressure, the French and the British pulled out from the canal, as did the Israelis. The Suez Canal returned to Egyptian hands, but they were forced to compensate the shareholders. Soon the Russians appeared on the scene, and it was they who built the Aswan Dam.

The Europeans continued to leave in ever greater numbers until the flow became an exodus. Relatives left, friends left, and then we left too. Only Egyptians remained in Alexandria.

Occasionally, we would come across an acquaintance from Alexandria and talk of old times. Out of simple curiosity, without nostalgia, we would ask, "Have you heard anything about Lysimachos?"

"Yes, he's fine. He's in Sydney now. He married Maro. You remember her, the athlete. They were going out together even back then. They've got two little girls now."

"And Stelios?"

"Who? The singer?"

"Yes, you remember Stelios . . . He loved to sing and tap dance."

"Oh, yes, Stelios . . . He's in Paris. He's a singer there."

And Pavlos and Dora and Costas, and Michalis and Fani . . . they had all been scattered around the world. Alexandria remained aside, off in a little corner of our soul, somewhat aggrieved that we did not think of her more, that we did not miss her yet.

Myself, I was caught up in far-away travels, I wanted to visit new countries, to assuage my voracious thirst to travel even further afield. Thirty years passed. Gradually, Alexandria began to creep into my mind more and more often. I missed the city. People I knew from back then who had not been able to stand the separation and who had gone back to take a look said, "Don't go back, leave well enough alone. Hold on to the memory of the beautiful city you used to know."

"Goodness, don't go back! It'll only upset you. You'll see an Alexandria so changed, unrecognizable. It'll only make you feel bad."

I hesitated . . . Perhaps, I thought, they were right. Perhaps I should keep that image of the Alexandria I had known. Or perhaps it was only a vision. Perhaps *that* Alexandria was nothing more than a figment of our imagination. Perhaps we had created her with myrrh, laurels, scents, imagination, and affection. "So let it stay that way," I thought. "For what will become of me if I am to lose the Alexandria of my youth?"

But, you see, the Great City had decided to take revenge upon those who had neglected her, and at night, as I closed my eyes, she appeared before me, insisting upon wandering with me around her streets and alleyways. She haunted my dreams.

Sometimes I saw her as she had been then, unchanged since we had parted. I strolled around the shops, the bazaar, I boarded the tram, I ran through the gardens with my grandmother, Sarandia, I went to the beach, I went fishing along the Corniche . . . At other times, my dream would become suffocating, nightmarish. I knew I was back in Alexandria, but it was terribly changed, unrecognizable. I entered a labyrinth of unknown streets leading nowhere. I searched for a point of reference, trying to orient myself.

"But where is Rue Fouad? Where is Attarin? Where is Ibrahimiya? How do I get to Ramleh Station?"

I tried to shout out loud, but no sound came out. I tried to stop passers-by and ask for directions, but they ignored me, and when I looked at them closely, their faces seemed to fade until they were just empty shapes. I would wake up deeply anxious.

Finally, I could stand it no more, and I set out for Alexandria. We approached the city from the desert, from that monotonous, interminable road. We passed Lake Maryut, the ancient Lake Mareotis, and suddenly we were entering the city on a road I had never seen before.

"Where are we going?" I asked myself. "Is this a new road?" We came out in Chatby. Suddenly the names of forgotten neighborhoods of the Ptolemaic era sprang to mind: "Soter, Cleopatra, Camp Cesar . . . "

"I'm near Ramleh Station already," I thought. "I'm back in Alexandria."

●

Today is the Bairam, a great feast. The fasting of Ramadan is over. The streets are full of people, just as they were back then. It is impossible to drive through the crowds. What a jam . . . I decide to continue on foot. I am moved to rediscover the Alexandria I once knew. I begin to recognize one building after another, and each of them has something to tell me, some memory from the past.

Blessed is the Great City: all the old buildings are still standing where I left them. Many have changed, have been transformed, but nothing is lost.

The streets are full of people, a cheerful, multicolored parade. You walk with difficulty, having to push your way through the crowds. The same *gallabiya*s, the same *milaya*s, only you do not see the traditional veil any more, and there are not many tarbooshes to be seen. There are very few foreigners about. People stare at me curiously. There are smiles everywhere, good-natured eyes. Here is the station where we used to take the tram. Just as it was back then, young and old hang in clusters from the wagons. The schools and the Greek Athletic Club at Chatby, the Corniche and the ancient port with the fort on the far side, are just as we left them, and the same waves still break against the same rocks. The cool breeze still brings with it that special scent that I have so missed. The Boulevard Saad Zaghloul, the great patisseries, the shops, they are all there, somewhat altered, somewhat aged, under new ownership. But still there.

We reach Attarin. There is the mosque with its tall minaret, standing on the ruins of the early Christian Church of Saint Athanasios. A little further on, the Orthodox Church of the Annunciation, across from the junior school I used to go to. And then the Catholic Church of Saint Catherine. But there used to be a small park here with tall trees where hundreds of sparrows gathered at dusk. The park is gone, along with the trees, which had seemed to touch the sky. The sparrows are gone too. What a shame!

If I walk toward the sea, I will come to Muhammad Ali

Square. But I am impatient to see our old *okella* . . . This alley must lead to Rue Salah al-Din. Yes, that's right, it's here . . .

Carnezis' bookshop has gone from the corner on the left. We used to go there every year when the schools opened to buy second-hand books. We were very careful with them so that we could sell them again at the end of the school year. So, Carnezis' has gone. There is a photographer's there now. What a pity. I would have liked to breathe in that special aroma of old books, aging on wooden shelves, mixed with the smell of pencil sharpenings, blackboards and chalk.

But the street is so narrow! Was it always like this? Did we just think it was wide? All the buildings around here are old—the newest ones must be at least a hundred years old. But they stand now, just as they did then, one next to the other, as if on parade for inspection. The buildings are worn now; it is as if they are embarrassed by their sorry state, as if they are ashamed that they have aged even more, that even more plaster has peeled off, that their innards can be seen through huge wounds—hanging shutters, gaping doors that can no longer be locked . . .

And there is the small mosque of Salah al-Din. It never did have a minaret. Who knows why. I had never really noticed before. Our building was right next to it. The upholsterer's to the left has made way for a car mechanic's workshop. What was his name, the upholsterer? He was a good man; he took such pride in mending those velvet-covered armchairs and settees.

I make to enter by the big, heavy, wooden door—it has lost all its windowpanes and has been left with the barred frames. Just at that moment, a crowd of little children gather around me to find out what I am looking for. They are all dressed up in their best clothes; some are wearing patent leather shoes, others are barefoot. The neighbors come out too, eager to help, without waiting to find out why I am there.

From the blinding light of the street, I enter the *bawwaba*.

The children follow like a flock of cheerful sparrows. As my eyes become accustomed to the semi-darkness, I begin to pick out the once-familiar surroundings that I had missed for so many years.

Then a hinge squeaks from under the staircase, a door opens, and out comes a dark, middle-aged man, somewhat squarish in build, with thick, short-cut white hair. He is wearing a white *gallabiya*, as is proper for a day of feast.

"Poor old Amm Ahmad is bound to have passed away by now. This must be the new *bawwab*," I thought.

I had to say something. I had to ask something. The *bawwab* was waiting to learn what I wanted. I mustered all the Arabic I could recall and said, "Many years ago, there used to be a *bawwab* called Amm Ahmad in this building . . . "

The dark, *gallabiya*-clad man looked at me carefully, moving aside so as not to be blinded by the light from the front door, and asked:

"And how do you know Amm Ahmad?"

The giggling of the children had roused the other residents of the building. We were surrounded by children and adults, all chattering away at the same time.

"Thirty years ago, I used to live here. On the first floor," I said, looking at the *bawwab*. He opened his eyes wide and stood there for a while open-mouthed like the victim of a stroke, or as if he had just seen a ghost. But he soon recovered and found his voice, mumbling in disbelief, "God of Mercy, it can't be true. The Greeks from the first floor are back! Welcome, welcome! Where have you been all these years? How's your father? Your mother? Your brother?"

He rushed from one question to another without waiting for an answer. He mixed his words with exclamations, gestures, and the rich Arabic terminology that went with such exceptional meetings: May the hour be blessed! You have cooled us with your presence! How bright is this day! And *sabah al-kheir*! And *sabah al-nur*! And *sabah al-full* . . . and on and on and on . . .

Seeing that I was standing there confused, he added, "It's me, Badri. Amm Ahmad's son, you don't remember me? You have forgotten me! I'm the *bawwab* of this *okella* now."

He picked two girls and a little boy out from the pack surrounding us and proudly announced, "These are mine. I've got others, older ones too . . . " And there, in the hallway, began an endless conversation with the gathered residents. They wanted to know where I lived and what I did for a living, while a few of the bolder ones even tried to practice the little English they had learned on this passing foreigner.

At the same time, Badri had begun a long monologue, attempting to fit all that had happened to him in thirty years into a few minutes and a few words. Without pausing, he opened the door to that little room into which I had never been, and putting his arm around my shoulder in a friendly fashion, encouraged me to bend over a little as I entered so as not to bang my head on the low ceiling. He offered me the only chair in the room and sat down himself opposite me on a bed that filled up the remaining space in the room.

Why, it's Badri! Suddenly I remembered. In all the years that had passed I had completely forgotten about him. Good God! I thought. This is Badri, Amm Ahmad's son. The little *bawwab*! Badri who I used to play with as a boy. Badri who was going to join the army and fight the Jews. Badri who had come with us to the gathering in Muhammad Ali Square.

The crowd of little children had now multiplied and filled up the whole *bawwaba*. Curiously they pushed to see who would be the first to get his head around the half-open door. Badri decided it was time to restore order. He stood up and, handing out light slaps, scattered the gathered children. The *bawwaba* was cleared of the little dark angels. Badri came back into the tiny room and opened another door at the back. It was then that my queries about how Amm Ahmad's large family lived in this cramped space were finally answered.

The second little door opened into the base of a lightshaft that had been covered over to form a room. The whole of the floor space was filled with mattresses. I noticed that there was another exit leading onto a small courtyard. It was from here that light came in and the children went out. This was Amm Ahmad's home. This was the home his son had inherited.

The second room was also used as a small kitchen. As soon as the door opened, a pretty, plump young woman in a blue housedress and a black headscarf appeared. She was young enough to have been Badri's daughter, but she was his third wife. Without explaining who I was, Badri asked her to make hot tea for their guest. I politely declined the offer of sweets, claiming that I had trouble with my teeth.

"You don't have to say much to women. You have to teach them to obey with just a few words, otherwise you spoil them . . . " I remember that wise Amm Ahmad had said this once. It seemed that his son was following his advice. He looked at me a little condescendingly, and said, "You only have the one wife?"

"Yes," I replied, "just one."

"I thought so," he went on, as if feeling sorry for me. "And have you got any children?"

"Yes, I have."

"Good. May they flourish. May Allah protect them. Next time you must bring your wife and children with you. I've got three wives, praise be to Allah, and good children. Four boys and some girls too."

He did not clarify just how many daughters he had. It seems that was not important. He was more concerned with the boys. Then he began to tell me about the old neighbors who I had forgotten about: when they left, where they had gone. He complained, "The Maltese from the second floor left after you, then the Greek teacher, then the Yugoslav with the Italian wife, the artist, then the Italian printer with the four sons—they went to Australia."

He sighed as he said this, and added from time to time, "Ah, what good times they were! Why did everyone leave?

We were so fond of you all."

I had no answer for him. I felt guilty that I too had abandoned the Great City that had given us all so much.

The steaming hot tea arrived, served in a glass, syrupy from so much sugar. As I sipped, I told Badri a little of my news. Then he wanted to take me up to the first floor, to the apartment where we had lived. He insisted.

"Let's leave it for another time," I said. "I'm in a hurry. People are expecting me—I really have to go." Inside me, a voice was saying, "Enough emotion for your first day back, you can't take any more."

"But you must promise to come back again."

"I will, Badri, inshaallah. God willing, I'll be back."

I left Badri with tears in his eyes. As he squeezed both my hands in his, I felt a tightness in my heart, as you do when leaving a good friend, a beloved friend.

Badri did not become an officer, he never did learn to read and write, he did not pull down the bronze statue of Muhammad Ali, and yet I felt a little jealous of him because together with Amm Ahmad's *bawwaba*, he had inherited Alexandria—his Alexandria and my Alexandria.

And so I left Amm Ahmad's son to watch over the *bawwaba* of the aging *okella*, my childhood memories, and my most cherished dreams.

Alexandrea ad Aegyptum

"Over there, on the shore beyond Ramleh Station, you could see the ancient remnants of the old city reaching right down to the sea. Next to the ruins stood a grand, majestic pharaonic obelisk of granite, and nearby, another stone giant lay slain and half buried in the sand. A little farther on, near the square where the statue of Khedive Ismail now stands, you could still see the toppled medieval walls of the Arab city.

"I was just a child then," Docteur Tawa went on, "but I remember it as if it were yesterday. Over there at Silsila, the ancient Cape Lochias, which we now call Kastraki—right there, where that fisherman is standing—were the ruins of a small fort. It's fallen into the sea now. The Franks called it Pharillon, because it stood as a smaller partner to the great Fort of Qaitbey on the other side of the Eastern Harbor, which was called the Pharos. You see, in those days, it was still remembered that on that rock the ancients had built the magnificent Pharos—the Lighthouse of Alexandria."

As he talked, Docteur Tawa gesticulated wildly in his efforts to describe adequately those long-lost ancient ruins that he had so loved, and his face lit up and became strangely animated. He often said that he accepted progress as something unavoidable, "which obliges us to make sacrifices," but that he was saddened by the destruction that had taken place "for no good reason and that could so easily have been avoided."

He had his own very special way of bringing back the past

at will, of bringing back those ancient ruins that he had seen as a child through the closing door of the departing nineteenth century. Tawa deftly straddled the years and sauntered through the Alexandria of the past with its fortifications, double city walls, and great gates. He could move from yesterday to today with the ease of a phantom, like a shadow from the past.

He would enter by the customs gate, the Gate of the Dogana as it was known, and he would stroll through the crumbling Arab quarter. He knew every building that had ever stood there and he could feel his way through their remains. He knew in detail what was to be found under the surface of the city too. He had studied the maze of the ancient water system with its two-story cisterns like great cathedrals with elegant granite columns and delicate capitals and arches.

Then he would leave those ethereal walls and saunter around outside the city in the shade of the palms where a caravan of lethargic Bedouins were watering their quiescent camels. And later still he would re-enter Alexandria through Bab Rashid, the ancient Canopic Gate, and cross the city until he came to the Western Harbor, the Eunostos. Docteur Tawa explained that Rue Fouad followed the same path as the ancient Canopic Way and to its left was the hill of Kom al-Dikka, the Paneion of the ancients, which was later topped by a Napoleonic fort. Farther on was Rue Nabi Daniel, which was said to occupy the same position as the ancient way of the Soma, where the splendid mausoleum of Alexander the Great must have been.

"Who can show me where Alexander is buried?" said Tawa in ancient Greek, his charming pronunciation echoing the question of Saint John Chrysostom fifteen centuries earlier. Even then, at the end of the fourth century, all traces of the tomb had been lost. Vanity of vanities; all is vanity . . . .

•

When I knew him, Docteur Tawa must have been over eighty years old. He had spent his youth in a very different Alexandria from the one I knew; a city that had not yet been deformed by the building epidemic. He would describe, almost tearfully, how at the end of the last century the tall buildings had begun to sprout, one after the other in great numbers, demolishing the remaining medieval walls and consuming whatever ancient and medieval relics they found in their path, almost as if they were set upon erasing all traces of the past, as if they were ashamed of the rubble that had accumulated as a result of earthquake, war, siege, revolution, and the depravity of man.

Nothing was left, of course, of the illustrious era of the Ptolemies, except for two pharaonic obelisks, the famous 'Pompey's Pillar' being in fact a Roman monument. But Tawa insisted that just a few years earlier you could see many wonderful ruins in Alexandria, witnesses of the successive civilizations that had blossomed in this narrow stretch of land between Lake Maryut and the Mediterranean: the ancient Egyptians had been succeeded by the Greeks, the Greeks had mingled with the Romans and the Copts. Later came the Arabs, who were followed by the Ottomans.

•

Let me try to describe Docteur Tawa—no easy task, for his is not a portrait to be sketched with a few simple strokes of the pen. He was called 'Docteur' because he was in fact a medical doctor, and a very good one at that, as indeed was his son Girard. His father, who had been doctor to the khedive, had sent him to study in Paris. Despite his great age, Tawa continued to visit the clinic every afternoon and to examine patients whenever his son needed a second opinion.

I remember that Tawa never used a stethoscope, but would simply put his ear to a white handkerchief that he had laid upon the chest or back of his patient. Holding his breath, eyes closed in concentration, he would carefully listen to the heartbeat, the workings of the lungs, the hidden breath of life.

Tawa's clinic was on the first floor of a beautiful building in Rue Sherif, where a long queue of patients would form every afternoon. They would wait on the stairs, sometimes right down to the *bawwaba* because the waiting room could not hold them all. Rich and poor, young and old, men and women from all the foreign communities of Alexandria, as well as Copts and Shamis, could be found visiting the good doctor.

The rich paid well for their consultation, but Tawa would not accept payment from his poorer patients. It was even said that on occasion, instead of accepting payment, he had actually given money to a departing patient. If the unfortunate visitor hesitated in embarrassment, the doctor would assume a serious air and pronounce, usually in French, "My dear friend, you must take the drops I have prescribed regularly, and drink a little broth in order to regain your strength. Off you go now, and I'll see you in a fortnight."

I do not remember whether Tawa was a Copt of a Shami mother, or a Shami of a Coptic mother, but in any case, he was a Christian. Bright and early on Sunday mornings, as we were setting out to go fishing, he could be seen on his way to attend the early service at the Coptic Church of Saint Mark.

Docteur Tawa was a good Christian, but claimed no monopoly on salvation for those of his own faith. Someone asked him once if only Christians would reach Paradise and the doctor replied, "My dear friend, it would be terribly egotistical of me to say so. I am sure that one can reach Paradise by many paths. And yet," he went on more quietly, almost as if talking to himself, "it depends, of course, upon what one means by Paradise."

•

Docteur Tawa spoke all the languages that one might hope to hear in cosmopolitan Alexandria in the middle of the twentieth century. It was not uncommon to find people who were multilingual in those days in Alexandria—apart from their own mother tongue, most people could converse in several other languages. Tawa spoke Arabic with that distinctive Shami accent that drags out the ends of words; his French was fluent like a Parisian's, and he could converse comfortably in Italian, English, and German, but he would get a little confused with modern Greek. He had some trouble distinguishing between the puristic written Greek and the spoken everyday demotic language. Docteur Tawa liked to say that he had been taught the language of Alexander and the Ptolemies by the great Alexandrian archaeologist of the previous century, Dr. Neroutzos Bey.

•

Although he had not formally studied archaeology, the doctor knew a great deal about ancient Egypt, but his great love was the study of the history and topography of Alexandria. He knew by heart the successive layers that had settled over the much-afflicted Great City through the years and he knew all the archaeologists who toiled to wrest her secrets from the depths of the earth.

Tawa lived two parallel lives: one on the surface of the city, where he observed that great melting pot that held the peoples of so many diverse nations at a time when the leaders were doing all they could to segregate them—no easy task after a century together in the same giant pot. Greeks, Jews, Armenians, Italians, English, French, Shamis, and Egyptian Copts and Muslims lived side by side as had their fathers and their grandfathers before them, each taking something from the city of Alexandria and each giving something back.

Docteur Tawa's other life was lived on another plane: below the burning asphalt and cobbled pavements, below the city of Muhammad Ali—here was a town inhabited by shadows of the past: Amr the Conqueror, the unfortunate Antony, the Ptolemies and their queens. From each period he took what suited him best and with those materials—stone, clay, memories—he created his own Alexandria, a fantastic city that nestles in the verse of poets and the writings of dreamers.

•

That summer Sunday morning, Docteur Tawa was trying once again to draw his companions into that different, utopian Alexandria of his. They were sitting on wicker chairs at a casino—the first one you come to as you leave the town going toward Ramleh. I should explain that a 'casino' in Alexandria is a seaside refreshment area, set on a platform stretching out to sea and standing on wooden stilts with the surf lapping below. Tawa's companions on this particular day were a Catholic monk, Frère Polycarpe; an Italian teacher, Signor Monticelli; and a Greek evangelist, Nicolas. They listened politely to Tawa, but it seemed that each of them wanted to lead the conversation in another direction. The monk was not particularly distressed by the disappearance of pagan temples, which he scathingly called 'temples of sin.' The evangelist had his own true path, had his own recipe for salvation, and anyway, was always prepared to disagree with the Catholic monk whenever his stance differed from his own. But the Italian teacher, a neophyte, newly posted to the technical school of Dom Bosco, had given up a comfortable life for the opportunity to come and live in this mythical city of Alexandria, and he listened with interest to the words of the wise old man.

At some point, Tawa realized that he had been so rapt in his passion for the past that he had not given anyone else a chance to speak. So he paused and looked silently out to sea, watching the waves as they approached and came crashing onto the sand. He began to sip his coffee with obvious pleasure, occasionally taking out a large white handkerchief from his pocket to wipe the corners of his mouth where his mustache met his sharp little white beard.

Talk started up once again but did not seem to be settling into a serious conversation. The men spoke of various topics: the last war, politics, Egyptian nationalism (which was on the rise), the departure of the Europeans from Alexandria. They nodded their heads. What would become of the whole situation?

"The good Lord knows," said Nicolas. "Difficult years lie ahead."

Frère Polycarpe agreed. He had lived in Alexandria for over half a century and felt that it was home. He used to say jokingly, "I am not French, I am an Alexandrian." He was deeply concerned that fewer and fewer youngsters were following the path of the Lord.

"There are just a few old monks left in the schools these days. You hardly ever see any young ones . . . "

The conversation moved on until the companions were discussing religion, God, and the nature of the soul. The protagonists of the conversation were the monk and the evangelist, but Professore Monticelli added, "It's a tricky subject."

He said this in French with a distinctive Italian accent. He spoke quietly, searching for the correct words, adding here and there the odd verb in Italian, quite sure that his companions would be able to understand.

"What is the soul? What do we mean when we use the word? L'âme . . . Does it have the same meaning for Frère Polycarpe, Docteur Tawa, Monsieur Nicolas, for me? Does Mahmoud the *bawwab* feel the same about the soul? What about Azdadzi the Jewish storekeeper and my landlady Roxanne, my uncle Cesare, Bogos the Armenian tobacconist? I'm sure that it means something different to us all. And yet the same uniform rule should apply, don't you think? Surely every soul cannot have its own laws, its own attributes."

"What is the *psyche*?" he asked again, this time using the Greek word.

Frère Polycarpe took it upon himself to reply—and woe betide anyone who wished to disagree with him, for he was

well read and was more than pleased to expound on a subject on which he was so expert. He quoted verses from the
Old Testament, the Gospel, passages from the Holy Fathers,
Acts of the Synods. Goodness knows how he remembered all
that! He supported his position well and dared anyone to
contradict him. Nicolas had his own opinion. Although he
had started out by agreeing with the monk, in the end they
disagreed on many details.

"But we all agree that the soul is immortal. It cannot be
lost, because it existed before birth and continues after death,
isn't that so?" said Tawa, and added with a shrewd smile, "It
is in my interest to believe so at my age, as I near the thresh-
old of the beyond . . . "

But quite what the 'beyond' held and how the soul would
cope with it was the subject of much debate. Each put forward his own view, apart from Frère Polycarpe and Nicolas,
who both took a noncommittal stance. However calm Frère
Polycarpe tried to remain throughout the exchange, he could
not hide his annoyance when his views were queried despite
the weight of argument he had put forward to substantiate
them.

"Anyway, gentlemen, we are all Christians, are we not?
What are we getting so upset about? The Scriptures are quite
clear: on Judgment Day, to the accompaniment of the trum-
pets of the archangels, the souls of the dead will be resurrected. Of this there can be no doubt," declared Polycarpe,
venting his frustration, crossing his arms and adopting once
again his usual calm air.

The evangelist was obviously not prepared to leave the
argument at that, but Tawa and Monticelli remained
thoughtfully quiet, wondering how such an obviously pro-
found topic had never occurred to them before. Tawa waited
for things to calm down a little and then asked, "Do you
know the story of the obelisks of Cleopatra?"

They all knew of the obelisks; they knew that the obelisks
had been sent abroad at the end of the last century and that

one was to be found in London, the other in New York.

"What have Cleopatra's Needles got to do with the resurrection of the dead?" scoffed the monk.

"Les aiguilles de Cléopâtre? Nothing," replied Tawa, "But, you know, looking out over there toward Misalla, I just remembered them . . . " And with a glance at the others he seemed to be asking, shall I go on?

It was the teacher who urged him to continue; being new in town, he did not want to miss this opportunity to hear such a story from one who had actually seen the monuments. The others said "Go on," but more out of politeness than interest, and Nicolas had a look that clearly said, "Who cares about a few old stones that aren't even *here* any more?"

•

Tawa began a short but well-formed introduction to his topic, taking his audience back to the end of the 1870s, explaining the difficult situation in which Egypt found herself as she attempted to be on good terms with the major powers. At the time, it was the fashion for foreigners to collect whatever ancient relics they could find while abroad and plunder them, taking them home to be shown in their own museums. The rapacious frenzy of these 'enlightened' Europeans ruined the antiquities not only of Egypt, but of Mesopotamia, Asia Minor, and Greece as well. Hundreds of mummies were removed from Egypt, violently torn from their eternal sleep; statues and offerings were taken from tombs; whole columns were shipped out.

About thirty years earlier, Muhammad Ali had offered one of the Alexandrian obelisks to England as a gift, and because the English had done nothing about it, he wrote in some annoyance to remind them to come and collect it. Eventually, the British government decided to send a ship with a crew of engineers and technicians to undertake the transportation of the huge granite monument.

Polycarpe knew all this, just as he knew that according to

the local tradition the monuments had originally stood before an Egyptian temple in Heliopolis and that five hundred years later they had been transported to Alexandria by Cleopatra, the last queen of the Ptolemies, to decorate the entrance of the Caesareum, the temple she had constructed in memory of her ephemeral lover.

The old doctor will drive us all crazy with his long-winded stories, he thought, a little vexed that the conversation had departed from its original course. He looked away to stress his boredom with the subject, but was quickly punished by the sight of an attractive, well-formed, young woman being swept onto the beach by the waves. She splashed around playfully, with the surf breaking against her thighs, and then stood up suddenly like a resurgent Aphrodite. She coquettishly pulled off her bathing cap, allowing her long black hair to fall free and to be blown about temptingly in the sea breeze. She certainly knew she was beautiful. As she basked in the warm rays of the sun, she gazed in the direction of the casino, well aware that eyes were upon her. The wet black swimsuit hugged her form like a glove, emphasizing her curvaceous body and making her appear almost naked to the hungry eyes of the clientele of the casino. With tantalizing flirtatiousness she began to dry herself off with her towel.

It was all Polycarpe could do to tear his gaze away. Repressed urges and unchecked desires were being raked up, voices that had not been completely silenced suddenly spoke, long-forgotten memories came rushing to the surface. She was sent by the devil himself, thought the monk. Cleopatra was just like that—sinful, infernal, and beautiful. She infatuated Caesar, Mark Antony . . . He crossed himself, kissing his holy prayer beads—the chapelet—with which his fingers played nervously, and turned away from the vision, to the west, toward the city. He tried to pay attention to what Tawa was saying, to drag himself away from the girl's wounding beauty, but what did he care for the dates and details that the doctor was still quoting?

God, give me strength, he said to himself, to escape the vision of that half-naked, exquisite sorceress. Deliver me from dreams—and save me from the boring, prattling stories of this senile old heretic.

•

The transportation of the fallen obelisk, weighing several tons, was an incredibly difficult task. The English had prepared a huge metal casket to hold the obelisk, which was to be launched into the sea and towed to its destination, the Thames.

"I didn't actually see all that," explained the doctor, "but I was told the story, and I even read it later in the *Illustrated London News*.

"It was here that strange things started to happen . . . During attempts to raise the fallen obelisk, the earth below it gave way to reveal a Roman tomb. The contents of the tomb included some offerings and metal weapons that proved the bones it contained to be those of a Roman soldier. One of the crew had the irreverent idea of collecting the bones and other contents of the tomb and putting them inside the cylindrical case together with the obelisk. This unusual vessel, which looked somewhat like a primitive submarine, had been given the nickname *Cleopatra*. But when 'Cleopatra's Needle,' together with the remains of the unknown legionnaire, was launched into the Eastern Harbor, the *Cleopatra* immediately ran aground. You see, the crew was ignorant of the ancient topography of Alexandria and didn't realize that in ancient times there had been a small island there called Antirrhodos. They had a terrible job getting her afloat again.

"You know, ever since I first heard this story, it has come to mind every time I go to a funeral and I hear the priest chant the words, 'I looked in the graves and beheld the naked bones and said: To whom could these belong? King or soldier, rich or poor, righteous or sinner? But give rest to your servant, O Lord, among the just as a gracious and a loving God.'

"Anyway, they eventually set off, but on the way to Gibraltar they met one storm after another. Passing through the straight, the tow ropes broke, as if the corpse of the legionnaire was loathe to leave the Mediterranean, was unwilling to enter the Atlantic.

"The crew struggled to resecure the *Cleopatra* to the ship. They began to complain and superstitiously to blame the series of misfortunes that had befallen them on mystical powers that were trying to prevent the expatriation of the soldier's bones. They saw bad omens all around them. Just a few hours out of Biscay, a terrible storm broke, with waves as high as mountains. This time it was the sailors themselves who were forced to cut the ropes connecting the *Cleopatra* to the ship as she spun madly, tossed by the crashing waves, and threatened to ram the ship. When she was set free and lost from sight, the sailors were satisfied that they were safe from the cursed vessel.

"'Thank God,' said the boatswain, crossing himself, 'and good riddance to her.'"

Frère Polycarpe crossed himself too, and glanced toward the beach. The cursed creature was still there, lying prone in the sun. It occurred to him that should he see this vision in his sleep it would not count as a sin—Saint Thomas had resolved that one. He felt a little better and devoted himself to the tempest in Biscay, the disappearance of the *Cleopatra*. He murmured, "May she disappear, damn her, and leave us in peace."

"But she didn't sink." said Tawa. "For a whole day and a whole night the crew battled with the waves and when the sea became calm again, there on the horizon was the *Cleopatra* floating calmly as if nothing untoward had happened. The only one who was pleased about this was the captain, who knew the trouble he would have had with the admiralty had he lost the gift of the khedive . . . It might even have caused a diplomatic episode.

"The ship approached the *Cleopatra* and the captain gave orders for the tow ropes to be attached once again, but the crew hesitated. The boatswain spoke for them all. 'With all due respect, Captain, we're not tying ourselves up to that cursed floating coffin again. She'll be the death of us. When we loaded up that dead Roman soldier we must have set free supernatural powers hidden in his tomb.'

"The captain was outraged. 'This is mutiny! I'll have you all charged as soon as we reach London.' He made a sudden move to reach into the drawer of his desk, but the boatswain saw what he intended and managed to slam the drawer shut before the captain could reach for his gun. The captain was silent. He looked nervously around to see who among his crew would support him, but some looked away and others were obviously taking the side of the boatswain.

"It was touch and go for a while—the crew were on the verge of outright mutiny when someone came up with a solution that would break the deadlock. It was simple—they should take advantage of the lull in the storm to send a sailor over to the *Cleopatra*. He would climb inside the vessel and remove the contents of the Roman legionnaire's tomb and throw them into the sea. They all agreed with this plan to rid themselves of the source of their bad luck. The captain himself raised no objection, but suggested that a passage from the Gospel be read as the body of the soldier was cast into the sea. The cook pointed out that the soldier could not have been a Christian—there had been all sorts of idols buried with him in the tomb.

"And so the wretched legionnaire, or what was left of him, was thrown without ceremony into a watery grave in the Atlantic Ocean, accompanied only by a few idols. The crew had calmed down and gathered on deck to watch the remains being committed to Hades for a second time. Then they continued on their journey, towing the *Cleopatra*, unhindered by further adventure, to their destination on the banks of the Thames, where they were met with pomp and circumstance. And ever since then, that slender Alexandrian obelisk has stood gazing at the gray London skies."

•

Tawa paused and looked toward Misalla as if he were return-ing from the rainy north to the sunny Great City of Alexandria. He sipped what remained of his coffee, wiped his lips, and continued before the others had a chance to comment. He looked Frère Polycarpe in the eye and said, "I try to imagine what will become of the bones of the Roman soldier on Judgment Day. I often think about it at night when I have trouble falling asleep. Sometimes I see a vision and, like a new John, I see the heavens revealed before me. I see archangels and saints, and angels accompanying souls back to earth, and I follow them. I look down from on high and see Alexandria, the place to which I am destined to return. The heavenly paths are crowded with countless souls recoiling endlessly from limbo. No one is exempt from this great call; everyone hastens to meet the promise of the Last Day. And then I hear a humming, a resounding call, not of birds singing but of a myriad cicadas chirping, and I say to myself, could there be a paradise without the call of cicadas; without the scent of *full* and jasmine and the sound of waves lapping the shore; without the footsteps of the poet searching for eternity?

"Looking down at Alexandria, I rediscover the treasures from my childhood that I had thought lost forever. But noth-ing is lost, everything is eternal. Look, I say to myself, this was Paradise all along! It is here, in this narrow strip of land between the reflection of the lake and the immensity of the Mediterranean—and yet it took me a whole lifetime to find it.

"A vast, exquisite picture lies before me—as beautiful and simple as everyday things so often are. I think, surely this must have been drawn by Chagall. Only he could depict human beings hovering as light as souls who need no wings. You see, the past meets the present and there is no future.

Time ceases to have meaning. The great hourglass that was placed on the Pharos of the Ptolemies will not be turned again. Today meets yesterday and becomes an eternal 'now'; we are freed from tomorrow.

"Generations of Alexandrians are resurrected: Copts, Romans and Greeks, Arabs, Jews and Europeans, Ottomans. But, how strange—it is not only the people who are resurrected, but the buildings that we had thought lost forever. Like dreams where anything is possible, the modern works of man are erased and the neighborhoods of the past re-emerge. We had never been promised such a resurrection in the Scriptures. We had thought the ruins were soulless, but now it seems that those works of men, carried out at the bidding of the gods, although they could not speak for themselves, did indeed have a soul.

"Great mosaics made up of priceless stones taken from generation after generation, and yet perfectly matching. The district of Brucheion is unconcerned by the presence of the Basilica of Saint Athanasios or the Serapeum rubbing shoulders with the Mosque of Omar, the steeples and the minarets in the neighborhoods of the Mouseion, the Timonium, the Caesareum, the Arsinoïon. They were all places of worship, weren't they? They were all inhabited by gods made in the image of man.

"The majestic avenues of Alexandria stand alongside the narrow alleyways of the Arab city, perfectly in tune with each other, enclosed as they are by the wild sea and mellowed by the desert. This is, I say, the Alexandria searched for in vain by the foreigners who have loved and praised her without knowing her.

"Alexandria is resurrected for all those who called her Utopia, who have loved her and lost her; the Alexandria of children and poets.

"And then I suddenly see the soul of the legionnaire among the silent hordes of other souls as he anxiously searches for his earthly body. He visits the Caesareum, seeking in vain for his earthly roots. He asks other heavenly travelers for directions—where should he go now that the time has come, the time that has been prophesied since the very dawn of creation?

"'Where are you from?' asks an angel who tries to help him. 'Tell me the name of your land and I will direct you.'

"And the legionnaire replies, 'Alexandrea ad Aegyptum.'"

•

Tawa closed his eyes for a second as if he wanted to seal what he had seen in his mind. He was tired.

The Italian teacher smiled, looked at Tawa and said, "That was all very interesting."

Nicolas, who had been listening intently with his eyes closed, now looked toward the city, shaking his head. Who knows what he was thinking.

Frère Polycarpe crossed himself once again, either to exorcise the heretical words of Docteur Tawa or because the enticing young bather had begun to walk toward the casino to collect her things.

"My dear friends," said Docteur Tawa, "it's getting late. It's time we were going."

The As and the Fs of History

When I visited Muharram Bey for the first time, nobody knew that ten years before, during the war, Lawrence Durrell had lived there. In those days hardly anybody in Alexandria had heard of Durrell.

My friend Debitondi, who had attended the Scottish school of Saint Andrews and who studied English poetry and literature for hours on end, was amazed that I had not read any of Durrell's work.

But how could I have heard of Durrell when at that time, other than some poems, only the first two of his island books had been published—the one about Corfu and the one about Rhodes. *The Alexandria Quartet*, which was to make Durrell famous all over the world, was written years later when he was living in the south of France.

Debitondi seemed disappointed by my ignorance, but he eagerly showed me to the Arab district of Muharram Bey. I had never been there before, even though it was close to the Cairo Railway Station and bordering on the European neighborhoods.

Among the clutter of mismatched buildings—old *okellas*, makeshift, ungainly blocks of flats, small stores, and workshops—you could make out disfigured old mansions, a sure sign that years before wealthy Europeans had lived in that part of town. We walked for a while until we came to number 19 Rue Maamoun, where my friend stopped in front of an old two-story building. It had a small garden dominated by huge date palms with pine trees growing in between. The neglected vegetation, left to its own devices, without human care, had grown wild and seemed to be struggling to climb the walls and the fence, to escape from the confines of the garden, but the roots, which had pulled themselves up out of the ground as if to see what was going on in the world above, would not allow it.

The shutters of the building were all closed and locked, a last thoughtful act of a conscientious servant before moving on to some new post.

The mansion stood deserted and alone, bemoaning its neglect, unfittingly attractive among the other unhandsome buildings, like an aristocratic old dame who must have been divinely beautiful in her youth, and who, abandoned in some retirement home, stands out from the other old folk in the dignity of her silence.

Debitondi pointed to a high octagonal turret topped by a small terrace surrounded by diminutive cement columns. There were four large windows that had once looked out over the street, but were now blind.

"Up there, in that little room—in that dovecote—Durrell lived and wrote for over two years during the war, from 1942 to 1944."

Later I learned that the passages he subsequently used for his Alexandria tetralogy were conceived there, in that mansion belonging to an old Alexandrian architect of Italian descent.

The house comes to mind whenever I read pages from *The Alexandria Quartet*: well-written text made up of beautiful words, carefully chosen, skillfully matched. But nowhere in the pages of *Justine, Balthazar, Mountolive, Clea* can I find the Alexandria that I knew, my city, the real city, the city that Durrell had promised us. Nor do I recognize his heroes as particularly Alexandrian.

I have met Justines, Melissas, and Nessims all over the world, real people, recognizable characters; *The Alexandria Quartet* brings them to a fantastic city—not Alexandria, but a

city imagined by a temporary resident.

You cannot come to know a city during war—she does not show you her true face at such times—and the Alexandria of the war years, the city that was inundated by thousands of foreign soldiers from the farthest corners of the earth, was changed, and for a while, was adrift.

But let us get back to Muharram Bey in the middle of the 1950s. We were not passing through that poor Arab district simply to visit the house where the later-to-become-famous British author once lived, but for my friend Debitondi to take me to a second-hand bookstore that I had never visited before. We got lost for a while in the narrow backstreets of the rundown neighborhood, dragged along as we were by the crowds.

Then we reached Hagg Ahmad's place. From the muddy pavement we descended three or four steps and suddenly, without warning, found ourselves in an enormous room full of books. Books everywhere, magazines, newspapers. Books on the shelves, books on the tables, books on the floor piled up like stalagmites of knowledge.

Hagg Ahmad's basement reminded me of the sugar tower in a fairy tale where everything is made of candy and chocolate, but in the fantastic underground world of Muharram Bey, instead of sugar there was printed paper in all forms, in all sizes, in all languages. Paper of all kinds and all ages maturing gently with the humidity of the Great City, year after year, unhurriedly, like a good wine in a cellar.

Although the door was always wide open, a distinct smell of old paper emerged from the basement, a scent common to all the second-hand bookstores of Alexandria.

Debitondi told me that Hagg Ahmad had many old and rare books and had recently acquired a portfolio of old maps by Claudius Ptolemy. I could not believe that such a rare work could be found in a shop in a neighborhood like this. So it was mainly out of curiosity that I set out for Muharram Bey, thinking, "Even if it is true, however cheap such books are in Hagg Ahmad's store, they will still be far too expensive for my pocket."

But my friend had been right! There really was a most rare edition from the mid-sixteenth century with reproductions of splendid maps by the Alexandrian geographer, and in excellent condition too. Hagg Ahmad was asking very little for such a scarce publication, but I had only just taken my first job and the price was beyond my means. I worked out that I would have to save up all my earnings for three years to afford it.

Of course, I was disappointed at this missed opportunity, but at least I was glad to have had the chance to browse those pages again and again, to carefully unfold the priceless maps, which Hagg Ahmad allowed me to examine without any objection.

But this edition was not the only 'treasure' in the shop—or perhaps I should call it a storage room. The things you could find there! From odd, enormous volumes of the *Description de l'Egypte*, Bonaparte's scientific expedition, to old Leipzig and Venice editions.

During the next two years of my life in Alexandria, I visited Hagg Ahmad's basement regularly, not so much looking for something to buy as for the pleasure of exploring the treasures that had accumulated there. I always left with some small, cheap book, which I often bought at the cost of forgoing my weekly visit to the cinema.

Hagg Ahmad and I became friends; our mutual love of books united us.

Was he very old, or did he just seem old to me? I was only twenty. He was not young, anyway. He was certainly a stout man, although I never actually saw him standing upright. He was always enthroned upon a low divan in a corner, from where he kept an eye on all the aisles leading to the single door of the shop.

He could have been paralyzed. He might have lost a leg . . . it was hard to tell because his dark *gallabiya* covered his lower limbs completely, allowing no scope for an indiscreet glance. Around him on the divan were numerous embroidered but soiled bolsters upon which he would rest his back, then, changing positions, would lean to the right or the left as if reclining on an antique banquet couch.

In front of him there was a *sufra*—a low table—where he would place all sorts of things: a glass of tea, his amber worry beads, his spectacles when he took them off, the fan he used to battle the heat with in the summer months, his newspaper, *al-Ahram*, which he scoured from front to back and which could, when elaborately folded, be used to swat flies.

I never found out how he got to the basement, or how he left. However early I arrived, Hagg Ahmad would be there recumbent on his divan. You might be wondering how he managed to carry out his business, how he found the books, how he sold them. Hagg Ahmad had two apprentices, two young Berbers, Musa and Khalaf; they did all the running about the shop, they were his legs. I must say that thinking about them now, their movements remind me of robots, which had not even been invented in those days.

However unbelievable it may seem, Hagg Ahmad knew where every book was in his shop. Passers-by did not stop in at his place; his customers were all regulars. Egyptians mainly, the occasional Greek or Italian. Usually elderly and serious, they either searched the familiar aisles on their own, or asked Hagg Ahmad if he had anything new in their field of interest.

"Indeed, Hamid Effendi," Hagg Ahmad would reply after some thought. "I recently received a very nice book on the inauguration of the Suez Canal." With just a glance and a subtle gesture, he would signal to one of his apprentices to bring the book. He would take it in his hands, tap it lightly between his palms to shake off most of the dust, blow on it a little. Then he would lean over the *sufra* to reach for his spectacles with their small, round, thick lenses and settle the flexible silver frames upon his perfectly round, dark, chubby face.

He would begin to turn the pages and, adopting a most serious air, the ritual of book-selling would commence. He started by turning to the back of the book, where he had marked in his own private code when he had bought it and how much he had paid. Then slowly he would come to the first page; he would admire the frontispiece and begin to praise the edition.

It is hard to say how well educated Hagg Ahmad was, but other than Arabic, he could certainly read French and a little Italian. He knew everything there was to know about each and every book in his shop.

The bargaining was usually brief and you could tell right away whether he was going to sell you the book or not. His original offer was usually close to the final price; Hagg Ahmad did not like bargaining, although this was the norm in the Levant. Unlike the other local tradesmen, who you had to haggle down to at least half their original price—and occasionally even half that—Hagg Ahmad would begin by asking a figure not far from the final one.

When he saw that he had a difficult customer on his hands, he would take the book back and politely but resolutely hand it over to Musa, asking him to return it to its place. And he would add, "I'm afraid . . . I myself paid a high price for it."

I had learned his habits, his ways of bargaining, and we communicated well. After much searching, I would come to stand before the couch where the bookseller was installed, with two or three books in my hands. I would give them to him and sit down in the wicker chair next to the divan. I began to praise a book even before he did so himself and as he turned the pages, I would talk about the book in question. "Do you remember, Hagg Ahmad, that last time I bought Alexandre Dumas' *Twenty Years Later* in the Nelson edition? Now, with *The Viscount of Bragelonne*—if you will sell it to me for a reasonable price—I shall complete the story of the Three Musketeers. How much do you want?"

Hagg Ahmad flicked through the pages in the usual way and stroked the elegant white binding and gold lettering. He put the volume down on the *sufra* and took up the second book by Mahmoud Bey al-Falaki, which described ancient Alexandria. He nodded as he browsed through it . . .

"Hagg Ahmad . . . there is a most attractive map inset," I added.

"Yes, I know," Hagg Ahmad replied, unfolding the map.

He took the third book, the guide to Alexandria by Breccia. Then he picked up all three volumes as if their total weight were significant to the price he would set. He seemed to be giving the matter careful consideration. Then he handed the books back to me one by one, saying, "Half a pound for the book by Breccia—did you notice that it contains three colored illustrations? One pound for the book by al-Falaki—it's rare . . . Twenty-five piasters for the novel," and as if regretting the disdainful way in which he had referred to it, added, "It's in excellent condition. As good as new."

"Hagg Ahmad, might I take them all for a pound?"

"No," he replied, and made to take the books back.

"Then what is your best offer?"

He flicked through them once more, as if painfully contemplating how low he could go.

"One and a half pounds for the three—is that all right?"

"That's fine, fine, Hagg Ahmad. Thank you, may Allah keep you well!"

Then he called one of the boys to bring an old newspaper to wrap the books up in and to make me a piping hot glass of tea. The money I had paid disappeared within Hagg Ahmad's ample leather wallet, which was stuffed deep into the pocket of his *gallabiya*.

The tea ritual was part of each visit to Hagg Ahmad's basement. He even treated me to a glass of tea when I did not buy anything. As I drank the steaming liquid, Hagg Ahmad would tell me a story. He was a good narrator and although he could be rather long-winded, going into great detail, he was never tiring. He enjoyed talking about the past and was always pleased to have an audience. I think I probably got many bargain books, less as a result of my negotiation skills than because I was willing to listen to the old bookseller's stories.

I heard so much from Hagg Ahmad: about his two trips to Mecca between the wars, which gained him the right to be called Hagg—pilgrim, that is; about Urabi Pasha's revolution, of which his father had told him; about the crimes of the sisters Rayya and Sekina that had shocked pre-war Alexandria. He often spoke of his father, Anwar, who had been King Fouad's head gardener at Montaza, and who had even known Khedive Abbas Helmi.

He talked emotionally about his pilgrimage to the Hijaz and the first time he faced the Kaaba in Mecca. This was the only story that he told over and over again, each time with some special detail to add, something significant that he had overlooked in the previous telling.

"In those days," he explained, "we used to travel on camels in long caravans. It was a difficult journey. Many never arrived, they fell by the wayside, but it was the will of Allah the Almighty that I should make the pilgrimage twice. Great is His Mercy!"

He did not say much about the Kaaba, the 'black stone' that fell from heaven, which is respectfully housed in the great square of Mecca, and he did not answer my questions about it. Either he did not know the answers, or he did not think it right to initiate an infidel in the supreme mysteries of Islamic doctrine.

He particularly respected Urabi Pasha, the nationalist officer who led the revolution against the rule of the foreign powers in 1882—the cause of the English bombing of Alexandria. He said that Egypt would have been different if that uprising had succeeded.

Of the crimes of Rayya and Sekina, two harlots of pre-war Alexandria who lured their victims to the notorious 'red-light' district of town, where they murdered and robbed them, he spoke as convincingly as if he had been an eyewitness. Whether there were thirty victims of the diabolical sisters, as Hagg Ahmad claimed, or fewer as I had heard from my mother, it would be difficult to say.

At other times, he spoke of his grandfather, who had been a gardener at Montaza, the summer palace of Khedive Abbas Helmi, and of his father, who inherited the post and later became head gardener to Fouad and then Farouk.

Many years later, when I visited Montaza, which had by then become a public garden, I understood why Hagg Ahmad had spoken with such admiration of that man-made earthly paradise standing so seductively lush on the very edge of the desert. Hagg Ahmad went to Montaza two or three times as a child with his father. He explained that 'Baba' lived in the staff quarters along with hundreds of other gardeners, laborers, waiters, cooks, maids, and housegirls who served the monarch, his family, and the dignitaries.

His father lived there with his fourth wife, while Hagg Ahmad lived with his mother, the second wife, in Muharram Bey. He never tired of describing the flowers, the trees, the sweet-smelling shrubs, the lawns, the *full*, and the jasmine. "Surely Allah the Merciful has made Paradise like this," he would say in the certainty that a place in the vast cool gardens of eternal rest was assured to him who had made two pilgrimages to Mecca.

He told me that one day as he was walking with his father along a remote path in the garden near the sea, suddenly Fouad himself appeared before them, strolling with his son Farouk. Hagg Ahmad, using all the richness of the Arabic language, tried to convey to me the awe he had felt upon seeing the king and his young heir.

Many years passed and the young prince became king, only to be overthrown in 1952 by the military *coup d'état*.

•

In 1956, after the nationalization of the Suez Canal by Nasser, Egypt was attacked by the British and French, and then the Israelis, in an attempt to reverse the situation. But it was too late, the hands of time could not be turned back; a short war followed, lasting just a few days, during which the British and French attempted a joint landing on the canal. In Alexandria we were surprised to hear the air-raid sirens again and to see British reconnaissance planes in the sky. The once-familiar sound of anti-aircraft guns, which had not been fired for ten years, echoed in our ears. The Europeans of Alexandria were afraid. English, French, and Jews hurriedly gathered up their belongings, sold their possessions for whatever they could, and left. A little later they were followed by the Italians and the Greeks.

A midday air raid caught me in Hagg Ahmad's basement. The bookseller's fear was great, his distress understandable. Those of us who had been through the bombings of the Second World War were justified in wondering whether the whole thing was about to start again.

Hagg Ahmad swore at the British, the Imperialists, and the *Yahudi*s, the Zionists, in terms as strong as his dignity would allow. But he also criticized Farouk, who he called an irreverent, irresponsible, good-for-nothing, and who he held to blame for all the ills that befell the land.

"But why, Hagg Ahmad?" I ventured to ask. "Why is Farouk to blame? He hasn't been king for four years now. He hasn't even set foot in Egypt. He's always either in Italy or in Switzerland."

"Ah!" cried the old bookseller, "You say that—but you don't know the whole story. All the evil that is happening to us and to our country and even to Farouk himself is written upon high," and, raising his eyes to the cobweb-covered ceiling, he repeated over and over again the word "*Maktub*" . . . that is, what is written, destiny.

"But please, tell me what you are talking about, Hagg Ahmad," I asked, with real interest. "I want to know what is written in the celestial book—it might affect my own destiny."

Hagg Ahmad ceased his fretting and settled himself on his couch. He slapped at the lad who rushed to arrange his cushions and sent him off to make more tea. Then he was quiet for a while. He put on his glasses. I thought he was going to read something, but it was just a nervous reaction, like the way he glanced anxiously from time to time toward the steps from where intermittent distant sounds of the anti-aircraft guns of Silsila came.

He looked at me uneasily, wide-eyed, the thick lenses of his spectacles magnifying his eyes so that they seemed almost ready to pop out of their sockets. He hesitated, as if unsure whether it were proper to entrust the commands of Allah to an infidel. But then, as if deciding to consider me as an Alexandrian, he began to relate a strange story.

•

"It must have been at the beginning of the century; Fouad had succeeded his father the khedive, Abbas Helmi, who had died. He himself held the title of regent and, although still subject to the sultan, was in fact preparing to declare the independence of Egypt and make himself king.

"One summer's evening as night was falling, Fouad was taking his customary stroll in the palace gardens of Montaza, with his aide-de-camp following at a discreet distance. Suddenly, inexplicably, an old woman appeared before him. The aide sprang forward to pull her away. But very calmly she told Fouad that she meant well, that she would tell him his fortune, his destiny. She spoke of many good things to come for him, his dynasty, and his people, provided that he and his family remained faithful to Allah and the commands of the Book, and that they used the letter F—the first letter of his name—as often as possible.

"Fouad was impressed by the words of the old soothsayer. He ordered that she be given a gold dinar and be well fed before leaving. It happens that my father—may his memory be eternal—who, as I have told you, was head gardener at Montaza, was near at hand and witnessed what was said. In fact, the aide instructed him to accompany the old woman to the palace kitchens. On the way there, she told my father: Your name is Anwar. Your father's name was Abbas, as Abbas was the name of his master, the father of our beloved monarch. For you and your family A is your lucky letter. Use it as often as you can in praise of Allah; you, your children, and your children's children.

"And then she sat, ate, and drank before departing, wrapped in her dark *milaya*. As soon as she had passed through the heavy garden gate, she vanished into the black of night.

"People heard about what had taken place. At the palace everyone was whispering about the Fs, but few were concerned with the As.

"A few days later, before leaving for his other palace in Alexandria, at Ras al-Tin, Fouad ordered some Italian artists to decorate Montaza with huge calligraphic Fs. Why did he choose the F of the Latin alphabet? Perhaps out of vanity, to imitate Napoleon, who decorated everything with his monogram, N.

"So F was carved grandly on the outer walls, F was painted on the gold-inlaid halls, Fs on the silverware, Fs on the fine porcelain crockery, Fs here and Fs there, Fs everywhere.

"Shortly afterward, Fouad's first daughter was born and he gave her a name beginning with F—Fawziya. His second daughter he named Faiza, the third Faika, the fourth Fathiya. Farouk was the fifth child, a son and heir, the pride and joy of the king. In the meantime, in 1922, Fouad had proclaimed himself king and declared independence from the Ottoman Empire, which itself had begun to crumble.

"The years went by. Fouad passed away. Farouk was crowned king and continued the devoted use of the letter F that dominated all the palaces. He married Safinaz and immediately changed her name to Farida. Farida gave him three daughters: Ferial, Fawziya, and Fadia."

•

Hagg Ahmad stopped. His mouth was dry. He sipped his tea and sighed sadly, "Ah!" before continuing.

"These last events were all in your time," he said, and indeed they had been, but I had never noticed the procession of Fs in the life of the royal family.

"All that time," Hagg Ahmad went on, "we—I mean my father and I and my two brothers—faithfully followed the commands of the Almighty as expressed through the words of that simple woman. We used up all the As in the glossary of boys' and girls' names: Ahmad, Abbas, Aziz, Ali, Anwar, Abduh, Awad, Ashraf, Aladdin, Ayub for the boys; Aziza, Aisha, Arousa, Aaya, Aida, Afaf for the girls.

"But things started to go wrong for Farouk in 1951; after his divorce from Farida he took a new wife, Nariman, but he did not change her name. He had strayed from the true path, seduced by sycophants, drunkards, and degenerates, first among whom was the Italian, Pouli, who he made a Bey. You must have heard about him . . . "

Yes, I had heard all sorts of terrible things about Farouk and his wild parties led by Pouli Bey.

"But the worst part," the bookseller went on, incensed, "was that a year later when Nariman gave Farouk their first son, an heir to the throne, they did not name him after his grandfather. Instead of calling him Fouad they named him Ahmad Fouad. The devil had succeeded in befuddling the king's brains and the Fs and the As were mixed up.

"From then on, everything went wrong," said Hagg Ahmad, and as if to agree with him the gunner of Kom al-Dikka let off a futile burst of fire into the clear blue sky, shattering the peace of the pigeons nestling under the balcony opposite.

"Ah, ah, ah," cried the bookseller once again, letting out a moan so deep that it seemed his very soul were escaping with it.

"Ah, ya Rabbi!" he repeated, calling upon the Heavenly Father in a way so convincing that it was as if at that very moment He were passing outside the door of the basement, ready to intervene like an ancient Greek god at the conclusion of a tragedy.

But nothing happened and Hagg Ahmad, to escape his fear, began a long monologue recounting the events of 1952–56: the abdication of Farouk in July of 1952, the proclamation of the newborn Ahmad Fouad as king, the exile of the royal family . . . all signs, he said, of their fate. Then came the appearance of an Alexandrian officer, Colonel Gamal Abd al-Nasser, as leader of the revolution. The abolition of the monarchy followed, then the declaration of Egypt as a republic, the nationalization of the Suez Canal, the Anglo–French intervention, the Second Arab–Israeli War.

There was silence. As the sun continued to shine high in the sky, the heat in the basement became more intense. The boys were sitting cross-legged on the bottom step watching the sky, eyes agog. As they sat quite still opposite one another, their ebony faces shining with sweat, they resembled the painted plaster statues of negro boys that were commonly placed in pairs by the entrance to the salons of bourgeois homes.

Hagg Ahmad silently removed his spectacles and rubbed the spot behind his ears where the metal frames had pinched. He laid the spectacles upon the low table and carefully wiped away the perspiration that dripped from his face, throat, and neck with a handkerchief so large that it was more like a restaurant napkin.

A horsefly resolved to break the silence, buzzing insistently around the room from corner to corner, from wall to wall. Hagg Ahmad folded his newspaper with careful, smooth, and graceful movements so as not to startle the fly. Then he waited like a primitive hunter for the insect to approach, to settle on the table, drawn by the grains of sugar scattered during the preparation of the tea. When the fly was within range of his swatter, Hagg Ahmad executed it with a sharp flick of his hand.

The silence had been disturbed, and Hagg Ahmad continued with the epilogue to his story. "When those who have been chosen by Allah to lead their people do not respect His wishes, then they are unworthy to rule and bring upon themselves, and unfortunately, upon their people too, the consequences of their impiety."

Even as Hagg Ahmad ended his narrative with these words of wisdom, a long wailing siren sounded the all-clear.

I stood up to leave and said goodbye. "Peace be with you, Hagg Ahmad."

"And peace be with you," he replied.

•

I left the dim basement and stepped out onto the street, into the savage sunlight. Blinded by the sudden glare, I squeezed my eyes shut. I saw stars, and among them on the horizon I thought I saw As and Fs flashing like distant comets. I was troubled by Hagg Ahmad's words and wondered, "How can a god play with the letters of the alphabet? Why should he test mankind with his mysterious ways? But then, who cares? What's it to me? I'll be going away soon. Just a few more days and I'll be leaving this flat city. I'll be moving on to new, distant places . . . " and as I came to a bend in the road I quickened my pace, all the sooner to leave behind Hagg Ahmad and his story.

A few days later I crossed other seas and arrived in a new land; I came to know other cities, which I thought were better than the one I had left behind. For many years Alexandria remained, for me, distant and forgotten.

•

In 1965 Farouk set out on his final voyage. His death was

recorded in a few lines in the small print of some newspapers. Perhaps Hagg Ahmad was already waiting for him on the opposite shore.

Another ten years passed, and ten more, and ten more after that. It was over thirty years since I had last been to Muharram Bey when one day I saw hanging from the front of an Athenian newsstand a French magazine that concerned itself with royalty, past and present. Every blue blood and aristocrat still clinging to worthless titles was packed into the richly illustrated pages of the magazine, to the relish of its readers, who gaped at the impressive garb of the men and the ridiculous hats and couture of the women, and who gobbled up the gossip columns like modern fairy tales.

My attention was caught by a photograph of a couple posing pretentiously on the cover. I stopped . . . "But that is Farouk," I thought. In fact, it was his son Ahmad Fouad, who, having reigned as an infant for ten months and twenty days, had attained the title of 'former monarch.'

I bought the magazine and sat at Zonar's Café avidly reading the sequel to the story of the Fs and the As.

The interview with Fouad was spread over several pages illustrated with numerous photographs. It seems he had abandoned his first name, Ahmad, and kept the name beginning with F. His wife's name was Fadila, their daughter Fawziya, their youngest son Fakhr al-Din. I began to worry about the future of the Egyptians, believing for a while that Fouad—who professed to the journalist that he was ready to serve his country whenever called upon to do so—had made amends with Allah and, faithful once again to the procession of Fs, was re-entering the broken line of the kings of the Land of the Nile. But I was soon relieved when I saw a photograph of Fouad's eldest son—he was named Ali, after his ancestor Muhammad Ali.

I had to laugh, almost out loud, attracting sideways glances from two elderly ladies elegantly sipping their sorbets.

How fortunate, I said to myself, that once again the devil has befuddled the brains of the king, has mixed up the As and the Fs and invalidated the prediction of the old sooth-sayer.

Are you listening to this, Hagg Ahmad?

How fortunate we are that in the face of the whims of the gods there are the ploys of the devils; it is, in a way, some kind of solution.

The Quails

Year after year, in autumn, as the first messages of winter arrive from the north, the quails set out on their great journey. They gather in the thousands, forming thick swarms, flying sometimes high, sometimes low, gliding over mountains, lakes, rivers. They leave in haste, restlessly beating their short wings, as if they are scared of the black clouds amassing, afraid that they might be caught on their way by the cold winter.

Year after year, they take the same, long path, followed thousands and thousands of times before. Many fall in exhaustion, drop behind, are lost. The others stubbornly continue their silent journey south, as the Creator ordained when He settled the things of this world. And they reach the Balkans and, as the quails know nothing of borders and the ways of man, they continue to fly. From high above they look down: rocks and more rocks. Scant plains, and all around as far as the eye can see, the azure blue of the sea; this is the land of the Greeks.

The quails know the paths of the sky well and they pass their secret message on from journey to journey, from generation to generation. Now they reach the rugged Mani; they enter by Porto Cayo. Do they know that the Venetians named it because of their passage?

Courage . . . they are almost there, a little farther on, just another stride, and Cape Tenaron rises up, that terrible headland abandoned from ancient times to legend and isolation.

They hesitate, they pause to rest a while before beginning

once again their interminable flight over the sea. They know that when they leave these woeful stones behind, they will find no place to rest until they reach the opposite shore, until they reach Africa. They survey the steep cliffs from above, the high towers, the stone walls, the rough, scattered, forgotten stones. Grass can be seen nowhere, with the exception of the deformed, twisted body of the prickly pear, blending with the landscape of stone. Rocks on one side, the vastness of the sea on the other, but the quails must rest a while in the scant shade of the prickly pear tree that thirstily suckles from the bowels of the earth. They must catch their breath before daring the crossing over the watery element. But down there is man, who, odd-looking, wild-eyed, has spread his nets out high, as if to entrap the very heavens: man waits for the passage of the quails.

Man knows that every year the quails will pass by this way, as is their custom. But the quails know too that men have set their traps and it is here that they will pay the toll set by the rules of the Great Journey. They know, because the quails were passing through this land before man had ever settled, and they will continue to do so well after man is no longer here.

The more tired among them, the weaklings, those who fly low, close to the rocks, will be caught, helpless, in the outspread nets. The rest, the majority, will continue to fly out over the sea. And the sea awaits them. Sometimes serenely feigning indifference, sometimes seethingly turbulent, as if she who is accustomed to the playful flapping of the seagulls is irritated by the quails' monotonous flight. And the sea will receive her sacrifice of wings and feathers. And the waves will take all those destined never to reach the opposite shore.

Those that survive the repeated batterings will see the Egyptian coast appearing suddenly before them on the distant horizon, like a hazy mirage, like a distant promise. Oh! How exhaustedly the winged travelers will fall upon the golden sands, eager to relax for a while, to catch their breath.

Of course, their journey does not end here, but a great barrier, the hostile sea, has been overcome, has been defeated. But once more, man is waiting, slyly, as is his way, with his nets outspread. So, after the endless beating of their wings, after a journey of thousands of miles, many will be trapped as soon as they first touch Egyptian soil.

•

Alekos walked slowly along the beach, along the uncertain boundaries between land and sea. He strolled alone. He stepped upon the wet sand, which held for a short while the imprint of his bare feet, the traces of his wanderings. But the next wave stubbornly erased them.

The sea, accustomed to her solitude, refused intruders. It was as if she were wary of humans, she who was more used to the companionship of the wilderness. Side by side with the sand, incessantly she caressed it. A little farther along were the sand dunes, following one another in disciplined order into infinity. Surely, thought Alekos, the sand dunes are trying to imitate the sea, the rise and fall of the waves.

He had been coming here for years. He used to come almost every Sunday once the weather got warm, from April to November. He would get into his old Citroën and set off toward the west, leaving the city behind, taking the road for El Alamein.

After an hour he would leave the narrow strip of asphalt road, which headed to Cyrenaica, straight as a line drawn with a ruler, and he would turn off down a sandy path. Carefully he would approach the beach. He would stop quite a distance from the sea so that the wheels of the weary old car would not get stuck in the soft sand.

He looked at the sea, then at the desert. They were so well suited. The sea, aquamarine, endlessly coming and going. The desert, staunch, immobile, pale, majestic, accepted the games of the sea, had grown accustomed to them with time, and had come to love her, even though he did not show it.

The waves broke against the shore rhythmically, again and again, letting out a tiny cry as they did so, conspiratorially cooling the burning sand before withdrawing, leaving behind a moist kiss. Not a seagull, a date palm, a blade of grass, a cicada dared to interfere with the lovers' games. Only the breeze playfully danced around and peeked occasionally, sometimes bringing the odd cloud along. You would see it approaching high in the sky, casting dark shadows upon the blue of the sea, and then it would move on to darken the golden sands.

The summer was coming to an end but it was still very hot. It was almost midday; the sun had climbed as high as it could and was hurling its vertical rays like burning arrows.

Alekos walked toward the multicolored umbrella that he had pushed into the hot sand. From a distance, he thought, it resembled a small flower in the buttonhole of a plain jacket.

He stepped where the waves broke, seeking some coolness. He had plunged into the embrace of the sea many times since morning, but as soon as he came out of the water the wild sun took over, sucking up the coolness and leaving a salty crust upon his skin. When he reached the shelter of the umbrella, he lay down in its protective shade. He closed his eyes. He relaxed, he felt good. He was enjoying the silence, the shady circle that spread out beneath the umbrella and the light breeze that came from the sea. He took a moment to listen to the sounds that reached his ears: the voice of the sea was omnipresent, chatty, murmuring continuously. Occasionally there came the roar of a passing car from the distant, roasting hot road. It did not bother him. In fact he found it comforting to know that he was not completely alone.

Suddenly he sensed something passing above him, and even though his eyes were closed, he felt that the sky had darkened. A flock of quails was passing hurriedly overhead. They tumbled exhausted into the sand dunes.

"The quails are early this year. They'll have a heavy winter in the north," he thought.

Then in his mind he made the migratory journey with them, the way he imagined it. He envied them, their passage through so many lands, while he, without wings, was bound to the dunes of Alexandria. It occurred to him that he had never traveled, not even to Cairo. The farthest he had ever been to the east was Abu Qir, where Nelson had sunk Bonaparte's fleet; to the south, to the shores of Lake Maryut where Edouard, the Armenian, had taken him duck hunting once; and to the west, to El Alamein.

El Alamein was just a few kilometers from where he now insouciantly sought his solitude. How different things must have been twenty years before. He tried to imagine the comings and goings of the troops, the tanks, the large lorries filled with soldiers, the roar of the cannons, the planes scouting that evening's target and the human beings who had gone out of their minds. He felt a sort of guilt, because he had not fought himself. He could have volunteered for the Greek army, as so many others had done. He had thought about it, but his mother had prevented him.

"How can you leave me, Alekos, my son? I've nobody else in this world. What will become of me if anything should happen to you? Don't do this to me, my boy," and her eyes swelled with tears.

Alekos did not say anything. He took shelter behind his documents, which declared no particular nationality, stating only: *nationalité locale*, religion: Christian Orthodox, of Greek extraction. He did not have a Greek passport, he was not registered in the records of the Hellenic Community or the Greek Consulate, so he would not be called up. Others would fight the war. He followed developments on the radio, in the newspapers, through discussions with his friends. He lived his war at night in the air-raid shelters where he had to drag his mother, against her stubborn refusal to go down into the *abri*.

He looked at himself in the mirror in the mornings as he shaved, saw his hair starting to turn gray, to thin a little, and he would justify himself by saying, "I'm not young any more. I'm over forty. Let the youngsters do the fighting . . . "

•

He looked at the sea, and then at the desert, then at the vastness of the sky. They all met.

Alekos used to come swimming here with Mary on Sundays. Right here, or perhaps just a little farther down the coast. They would be alone. They would put up the umbrella and plunge in and out of the sea, then lie in the sun and make dreams . . . When they had first come to this isolated beach it had been at this time of year and the quails had passed overhead. Mary talked about the quails. She spoke so beautifully about small, simple things. That was years ago—so many years had passed since. Alekos tried to count: "Yes, it was after the end of the war. It must be ten years."

Alekos counted the years that passed, marking them with various events.

He used to say, "It was five years after the end of the war when I met Mary, it was in the autumn of 1950."

"We started coming to this beach two years later—in the summer of 1952—when Farouk was deposed."

"Mary and I split up in 1956, the year that Nasser nationalized the canal."

In 1936, when the Olympic Games were held in Berlin, Alekos felt for the first time the fear of time passing. It was as if he had climbed up a high hill and when he reached the top he looked down the other side and saw death waiting. Then he realized that half of his life was gone. He had arbitrarily decided that he would live seventy-two years. He was scared—the years he had lived seemed too few, far too few. "But I have as many left to live," he said, to console himself, though the thought did not satisfy him.

Now, as he watched the quails passing in waves, he began again to make his ominous calculations. He reflected, "It's five years since Mary left. I'm sixty years old now, so I've got roughly another ten years left . . .

"This time last year, my mother died. She was very old, she was over eighty . . .

"Who knows?" he murmured. "Maybe I'll reach her age." But he did not really believe he would.

It was terribly painful to lose his mother, Kyra Malamatenia—he had adored her. She had brought him up alone, as she had been widowed young. He felt so alone now. He who was an only child, a loner who had few friends, who avoided crowds, company, noise; it had scared him to lose his mother.

His best friends had left a long time ago—Edouard, who took him hunting from time to time, had gone to Canada. Elie, the Jew, with whom he used to go to the Fouad Cinema every week to see French films, had emigrated to Tel Aviv. Costas and Michalis, who had been fellow athletes at the Greek Athletic Club, had started new lives—one in Australia, the other in Brazil. They had married, they had children, they were successful . . . Foni, Costas' sister, who used to read Cavafy's poems out loud, had married a left-winger in Greece and was struggling from exile to exile, trying, as she said, to make a better world.

"Memory—what a terrible thing memory is. A blessing or a curse? A blessing and a curse." Once some friends had been discussing what was the most valuable thing we have, and what would be the most frightening to lose. Some had talked about people, others about ideas, values—hypocritical words, made-up words; someone talked about life, another about sight . . . When it was Alekos' turn to speak up, he answered without hesitation. "Memory. If I were to lose my memory, I would lose everything. I would lose my past and I would have no future . . . I would cease to exist."

Was he right? He remembered his Uncle Alexandros, who had completely lost his memory for years. In the beginning, he forgot recent events. As if nothing was being recorded any more inside him. He would say the same thing over and over again. He would set out to go somewhere, but would come home confused because he could not remember where he was going. He would greet someone, and then a little later would greet him again, and then again, as if he were meeting him for the first time.

He repeated the same thing time after time. The same stories about the past, which he remembered in every detail. Like the worn-out tale he told about the time, in 1882, when he had seen Urabi Pasha on a white horse, wearing a red fez, with epaulets braided in gold and a shining sword. Then he would describe the bombardment of the city by the English fleet that followed the slaughter of the Europeans by the locals. It was as if he were reading it from a book. He related it all without leaving out anything, all in the same order as he had said it before: how many English ships there were, how many Egyptian batteries in the ruined fortifications, how many days the bombardment lasted.

Later, as the years passed, starting with recent events, gradually all his memories were erased. He remembered nothing. It was as if he had never lived. His life was like an ancient palimpsest, a manuscript from which the inscriptions had been scratched away in order to economize on parchment or papyrus. Uncle Alexandros was an ancient palimpsest from which all previous writing, all previous records had been erased. He was empty, and only from his age, from the faint imprints that had not been completely lost, could you sense that Uncle Alexandros had ever lived. Sadness, joy, hope, and disappointment had been scored upon his wrinkled face. But in his memory everything had been carefully obliterated. It had been erased by the invisible hand that decides the fate of man; or perhaps unintentionally by a mere coincidence, the act of a careless god, as an absentminded passer-by obliviously destroys the labor of ants.

In every other respect, Uncle Alexandros was in good health. Nobody could remember him ever being ill. He ate, drank, went out for walks, flicked through the same magazines again and again, for hours on end. He saw the same pictures over and over, but nothing was recorded anywhere. One evening, in his sleep, he passed away, just like that, without even realizing it.

"Could it be that perhaps Uncle Alexandros was happier than any of us," Alekos mused, "spending as he did the last years of his life without a memory? Who knows. Those last years are so difficult to live . . . "

But he was terrified by the thought of losing the memories that he had carefully filed away inside his soul. In one drawer of his mind, which he tried to keep hermetically closed, he hid away all he remembered of Mary. The memories of those beautiful moments that they lived together were so painful, and now that he felt he had lost her forever, he avoided bringing them out. He had never dared to face the reality of their separation; just as he had been afraid to look upon the dead face of his mother and had avoided doing so, he could not come to terms with the fact that he had lost her too forever.

But through the cracks in the closed drawers, images escape as exhalations of the past, they nest inside us, we push them away because we do not want to feel the pain, but they tenaciously circle again and again, waiting to possess us.

The sea, the sun, the burning sand, the shade of the umbrella, the flight of the quails . . . he could not resist. He closed his eyes again and gave himself up once more, after so many years, to Mary. He allowed her vision to capture him.

He returned to the years just after the war when, one winter's Wednesday, late in the afternoon, he knocked upon the door of the ground-floor flat in Mazarita where she lived. He remembered that it was raining and fat raindrops beat rhythmically upon his open umbrella. It took a long time for the door to open . . . Out of his pocket he took a crumpled piece of paper on which Stergios, the clearance agent's clerk, had written the address. This was the right door. His heart was beating hard; it always beat like that when he first met an unknown woman. Might it be that Stergios had forgotten to let her know he was coming?

The door opened; for a moment Alekos was taken aback. He had not expected her to be so pretty . . .

He remembered every detail of the following two hours as if it were only yesterday: what Mary was wearing, how she had combed her short, black hair, with a fringe over her forehead, her perfume, which made him giddy whenever he approached her, the few whispered words that came out hesitantly, the unfinished sentences that left her succulent lips half parted, the cigarettes they lit one after the other and extinguished before they had burned halfway down. But above all there were Mary's eyes, those enormous black eyes that looked at you so sadly, even when they tried to smile. He could make them out even in the semi-darkness when Mary threw a translucent shawl over the lamp on the bedside table to dim the indiscreet light. Those enormous eyes, with their black, arched brows accentuated in dark pencil, reminded him of the portraits of Fayoum. Later, she turned the light out completely, and for a while all that was to be seen was the glowing tips of their cigarettes, burning brighter then fading, following the rhythm of their breath. When she turned the light back on, he paused to look once more at those eyes. They drew him into their dark depths, like a whirlpool, and held him captive.

"My God," he whispered, "You are so beautiful . . . "

As he left, he said, "I'll be back next Wednesday."

He said this hesitantly, as if unsure whether she would agree. She smiled and said, "Wednesday. Same time."

The rain had stopped, the road was shining as if it had just been freshly coated with pitch, and here and there a weak streetlight was reflected in its surface. He walked to the nearest tram station with slow strides. He was almost there when he saw the tram approaching. If he had quickened his pace, he could have caught it, but he did not feel like hurrying. He let the tram go without him. He decided to walk a bit.

The evening was dark, the sky covered in heavy clouds. A mantle of humidity and darkness hung over everything. He reached the Greek Athletic Club. It was deserted. He kept walking toward the gardens of Shallalat. His footsteps echoed as he walked blithely down the middle of the road. He enjoyed the rhythmic sound of his heels. Tac . . . tac . . . tac. And he added another light 'tik' as he tapped the point of his folded umbrella, as if it were a walking stick. He passed in front of an ancient ruin, a remnant of the Canopic Gate, the only relic of the old fortifications of the city still standing.

He felt so good. He could not explain why. Stergios had told him that 'the girl' was very beautiful . . .

He began to count the days. How slowly they passed . . . On Wednesday, at the same time, that time when the day prepares to surrender to the night, Alekos rang the bell of that same door to the ground floor-flat of the small *okella* in Mazarita.

Later, as he was leaving, he said, "I'll see you again, on Wednesday . . . same time."

"Fine, Alekos. Good night."

Now the week was sweetly revolutionized. Before, the weekly milestone had been Sunday, and when Wednesday came, Alekos counted that as the middle of the week. Now the week was cut in two, and like an initiate newly privy to age-old mysteries, he awaited impatiently the weekly ritual of purification. Weeks passed, months passed. The winter passed and suddenly, as is usual in those parts, summer arrived.

Every Wednesday, Alekos took the same road, rang the bell of the same door, but now the days were longer and sometimes as he left, the sun was still shining on the Corniche. He had learned a lot about Mary, but he hungrily tried to learn more every time he saw her.

She had married at the age of twenty, a few months before the outbreak of the war. It was an arranged marriage with a sailor. There were only a few sailors from Alexandria. His name was Takis. They were about the same age. Then the war came. Takis' ship was one of the first to hit a mine off Malta. It went down with all hands. The whole crew was lost, and with them the newlywed little sailor.

Mary cried more for the loss of that young life than out of love. They had not really had time to get to know one another. Her mother was inconsolable. She was a widow, and she had only just thanked God that she had managed to marry off her daughter . . . "What curse is this upon us!" she repeated over and over again.

Mary wore mourning-black for a whole year. She worked with her mother, who was a seamstress. These were difficult, complicated years. The city was adrift; it had lost its rhythm. It had been taken over by soldiers of all sorts—sailors, airmen from distant countries. They would come and go, stay a while to rest between battles, to try to forget the horrors of war, and then return to the decks of their ships, the cockpits of their airplanes or the uncomfortable space in the shade of the cannons.

Suddenly, her mother died of pneumonia. She lost her in just a week. She dressed in black once again. She was alone. She worked all day and all night in an effort to keep her mother's clientele. Another year went by like that. It was the autumn of 1942. The war was raging. The battles reached the gates of the city. There was fierce bombing at night. The Germans were getting closer. And yet the city refused to sober up. The partying continued. The troops who arrived on leave from the front wanted to have fun, to drink, to enjoy every earthly pleasure to the last drop.

"Who lives, who dies? This might be our last leave . . . "

Behind the heavy, dark curtains of the blackout all sorts of nightclubs operated: bars, dancehalls, cabarets, clubs. You could hear the drunken soldiers singing in howling voices—Yuppee-ya-ya, Tipperary—indifferent to the planes above taking aim on the Great Port. Staggering, they left in groups at the first suspicion of dawn. English, Australians, New Zealanders, Scots, South Africans, and the allies who had escaped the occupied lands of Europe—accompanied by all kinds of girls: skinny English girls, cheerful chubby Greeks, short Maltese, shy Jewish girls, while the more daring soldiers set out for the Arab districts in search of local pleasures, defying the MPs patrolling the perimeters of the 'out-of-bounds' areas.

All wars set free occult powers: the powers of good and the powers of evil, ingredients of man's soul that coexist and collide within us.

Pitsa, a lively divorcée, a customer of Mary's, suggested that they go out one evening to dance at the English officers' club. Mary was hesitant at first, but then she thought about it and said, "Yes, Pitsa, fine, I'll come and have some fun. I can't stand this miserable life any more."

They painted the town red until the early hours. Pitsa, who spoke a little broken English, introduced Mary to her friends. Mary stood out from the other girls; she was very beautiful. They argued over who would get to dance with her first, who would buy her a drink. As the night went on, the partygoers got more and more drunk, the club got noisier and noisier. Finally, there was some sort of misunderstanding and a fight broke out between two petty officers of the Royal Navy. There was a right to-do. Pitsa was used to this behavior and just laughed, but Mary was frightened and wanted to go home.

In the end, Johnny Brown accompanied her home. He was a short, stocky, Welsh chief officer who was staggering a little less than the others. The next day, he managed to find her flat again, and in the late afternoon he arrived on her doorstep, freshly shaven and sober, and rang the doorbell. He had brought with him two very welcome paper bags containing tins of corned beef, some chocolate, a bottle of whisky, and some cigarettes from the NAAFI.

Johnny's ship stayed in port for another month, and then

he left . . . He never came back. Mary continued to go out to various armed forces clubs at night. She sewed fewer dresses, and when, toward the end of the war, Alan, a sergeant with the British Forces permanently based at Alexandria, asked if he could rent one of her spare rooms, she accepted readily. Alan paid well, more than the two pounds a month which the room was worth. Of course, Mary cleaned and cooked for him when he was home, but he was also good to her, he looked after her.

The flat in Mazarita contained all one could wish for. Not that anyone in Alexandria had to do without the basics during the war, but whoever had access to the British Army Stores could get tinned food, English chocolate, real Scotch whisky, Players cigarettes with the bearded sailor on the lid of the tin, and nylon stockings. Alan even brought her silk from a parachute one day so she could make it into sheets.

Mary had a good life—just as so many others had made themselves comfortable because of the war. And who cared . if the old maids from upstairs scowled at her? In any case, wasn't she helping, in her own way, to raise the morale of the allied troops?

In those days all sorts of things went on and much was said about the ladies and girls of the foreign communities. As Alekos' mother used to say: "What's the world coming to . . . My God, what'll happen when the war ends?" Because the wives whose husbands were away fighting were not all virtuous, and neither were the Italian wives whose husbands were interned all Penelopes . . . Strange stories were told about Italian women who were having affairs with English or Maltese men . . . That is, not only were they cheating on their husbands who were roasting in the internment camps at Fayed, but in a way, they were collaborating with the enemy.

"There'll be blood shed for honor!" Kyra Magdalene shouted so as to be heard by Irma who lived across the way. "Just wait and see what'll happen when the war's over and the poor cuckolds come home . . . "

Luckily, Kyra Magdalene proved to be wrong in her predictions. Nothing happened after the capitulation of Germany. The only consequences, at least the only visible ones, were a few hasty marriages between English and Greeks, and even with Italians and Maltese.

The deceived husbands were satisfied to come home. Those who had fought said to themselves, "Thank God I got home safely," while those who had been interned rediscovered the comforts of home after the hardship of the camps and decided to be understanding. "What's done is done . . . "

The arrival of blond children was justified by the fact that their great-grandfather had been blond and had had blue eyes . . . even blond Egyptian children with tight curls found warm affection in the Great City, the city which could tolerate anything, and cover up everything.

Many had not come to terms with the fact that the war would end some day, that this crazy interval would pass. They were surprised when it happened and wondered what they would do without the war.

But Alexandria did not return to the way it was before. For everyone, something had changed forever; the innocence of the lost paradise had come to an end.

For a few more months the sergeant stayed on as Mary's lodger. And then he left too, returned to Cornwall, where he had a wife and two daughters. Mary knew about them; he had shown her the occasional letter and photographs of the girls. Alan was a good man, quiet. He was affectionate. He felt sorry to leave her. Pitsa eventually married Bobby, an Englishman with the Royal Navy, and went to live in Cyprus where he was now serving. The Egyptians did not want the British bases. The English packed up and moved out to the canal.

Mary thought of going to Athens, where she had an uncle and some cousins . . . then she met Vivante, a Jewish merchant who had a nice corner shop selling women's clothes on Boulevard Saad Zaghloul. He had been a widower for many years, a womanizer, they said. They saw each other twice a week.

•

Alekos opened his eyes. The glare of the sun blinded him. Many years had tumbled all together and now he found himself once more on the beach, with the azure blue of the sea before him. He wondered, how many images can fit into the human brain in just a few seconds? In the blink of an eye, years pass, whole decades.

"Why am I bringing all this back?" he said to himself, moving his lips as if asking the sea this question. But she indifferently continued her monologue.

The foreigners had slowly begun to leave the city, although there were still several tens of thousands of them. The most numerous were the Greeks. Their community was tightly knit, tied to its clubs, associations, families, friendships; almost everyone knew everyone else.

Many people knew many things about Mary, which was why Alekos, even though he now had a close if strange relationship with her, hesitated to ask her to go out with him. Where would they go? To the cinema? People would recognize them . . . If they went to the Athenaios to dance one Sunday evening, the next day there would be gossip. Should he take her to the Greek Athletic Club? Now *that* would really cause a scandal.

And would Mary want to go out with him? However much it hurt to face the fact, he knew that he was just Wednesday's visitor, and there were seven days in the week . . .

One Wednesday evening, about a year after they had first met, he asked her, "What do you say we go out on Saturday evening?"

"Alekos, dear, I'd love to," she replied, and her eyes filled up with tears of emotion. But she did not seem surprised; it was as if she had been expecting him to ask for a long time.

It was already dark when they set off. Walking side by side, they reached the Corniche. They walked along the coast toward Silsila, the cape that closed the ancient port to the east. They passed by the barbed-wire fence—it was still a forbidden zone—where some old anti-aircraft cannons were set up and an Egyptian soldier armed with gun and bayonet patroled lazily up and down.

They continued their evening stroll. There were few people on the street here; the crowds were on the other side, at Ramleh Station, on the boulevards, in the pastry shops, the cinemas, sauntering up and down, gazing in the shop windows of the large stores.

A little boy with a basket of sweet-smelling *full* and jasmine ran up to sell them some flowers.

"Buy a bunch, sir, for the lady."

Alekos placed a garland around Mary's neck and handed her a posy of *full*. She took his arm and squeezed it tightly in thanks. Then, as if forgetting to remove her hand, she continued to hold onto his arm. Was it the scent of the *full*, which mingled with the fragrance of the jasmine; was it the beauty of the evening . . . ? Alekos felt good. He thought he had never felt so good.

That secret evening stroll was followed by more of the same. Then Alekos became braver and suggested that they go to the cinema. They went sometimes to the Metro Cinema, sometimes to the Amir. They avoided going in when the lights were up, making sure to take their seats in the semi-darkness, just before the film started. They were always the last to leave. Sometimes after the cinema, very late in the evening, they would stop at a brasserie for a glass of Stella beer and something to eat. They were less cautious now . . .

They saw each other almost every day. Giving up one by one her regular and ephemeral relationships, Mary dedicated herself to Alekos. Kyra Malamatenia realized that something had changed in her son's behavior; his habits had altered—he was at home less, he came in late at night and occasionally, on the pretext that he was a guest at the Mesina chalet in Sidi Bishr, he would stay out all night. She did not like all this. Sometimes she spoke to him of marriage, without really believing it. Usually at New Year, Easter, on his name-day and birthday, she would make a wish for him: "This time next year, may you be married." And sometimes she tried to make a match for him.

"Do you know who came asking about you the other day, Alekos?"

"Now, how would I know," he replied.

"Harikleia, the French teacher." Harikleia had given Alekos private French and piano lessons some thirty years before, and she dropped in to visit Kyra Malamatenia from time to time.

"She was telling me about Themistoklis, a neighbor of hers. He's a teacher. She says he has a first-class daughter, a good housewife, beautiful, young, and from a good family . . . You remember her—Froso. We saw her last year at the Resurrection service at Saint Saba . . . Oh you do . . . Froso, the one who was afraid of the firecrackers and kept coming to stand by you . . . "

"Oh mother," he replied with a sigh. "Don't you ever tire of matchmaking? I remember Froso, but how would that little girl suit me? There's a time for everything, and when it was my time to marry, I didn't. It's too late now."

"Shush, son! What nonsense! Haven't I told you about your grandfather who was over fifty when he wed and went on to have five sons?"

"Yes, you've told me, mother," said Alekos, laughing, "but you forget that Grandfather Theocharis remarried at fifty after he was widowed because he needed someone to bring up his three daughters by his first wife."

"What's that got to do with it?" said Kyra Malamatenia, giving up the discussion.

Why had he remembered Harikleia and Frosaki, who blushed whenever he looked at her . . . ?

If I had married little Froso, surely I would not have met Mary. That's life . . . Forked roads are always appearing before us, and we must choose which route to take: Right or left? This way, or that?

He recalled the summer Sundays when he and Mary had begun to go to swimming. They would come to these isolated, quiet beaches near El Alamein, sure that they would not meet anyone they knew, as nobody ever came out this way.

In those days the first two-piece swimsuits were timidly making their appearance in Alexandria. They were called 'bikinis,' although they bore no resemblance to the provocative bathing costumes of the same name. For Alexandria, though, they were considered scandalous and were strictly forbidden on the beaches. If some bright young thing wished to wear a bikini, she had to go outside the city, to an isolated beach, to Agami or Maamoura.

Bringing all this back to mind made Alekos nostalgic. It hurt. He carefully considered the past, he put aside the things he would not do again if he had a second chance. The images came into his mind, jostling each other in no particular order, some fragmented, some complete.

He tried to pause at that spring evening that had indelibly marked the rest of his life. Until then he had not wanted to look at the images of that day; they hurt too much, he avoided them, and when they came to him sometimes he would shove them aside hastily. But today he had decided to face what had happened, to look at the images, and they came to him and he surrendered to them . . .

When was that afternoon that we went to the Flower Festival? It must have been in May 1956 . . . yes, it was then, a few months before the nationalization of the canal.

Why had he decided to do it? How had he dared . . . ? He knew that the whole of the Greek community of the city would be gathered at the stadium. Scores of carriages paraded every year, decorated with a myriad of multicolored flowers, adorned by the prettiest girls in the city. Music, songs, and revelry in the evening, dancing until dawn on the open-air terrace of the Athletic Club, which adjoined the stadium to the west.

Mary had asked him hesitantly, "Have you really thought this through, Alekos? Are you sure you want us to go to the Flower Festival?"

"Yes," was his reply, abrupt and stubborn.

He knew that they would be exposed to a wave of gossip . . . You see, respectable society did not put up with such provocation. Some exceptions were made, of course, as long as the war lasted, but afterward everything had returned to normal.

Yes, Alekos had thought it through. For days he had been struggling with this idea of a public appearance. He always made his decisions alone. He had talked it over with himself at night before going to sleep. He was not used to opening up to friends; he did not ask for the opinions of others, for advice.

And why not, if you please? he said to himself. Am I answerable to them? I don't need them anyway. Why should I worry about what they think or what they say? I don't have to explain to anybody what I do . . . who I go out with, where I go.

He had gotten himself all worked up now.

And even if I wanted to marry her . . . then I'd marry her. I don't have to ask anyone's permission—well, I'd have to ask my mother, of course. She's the only one who has a right to give an opinion.

The idea that his thoughts had gone so far scared him.

All right, so I'm not going to decide that today. We'll just go to the Flower Festival . . . and if they don't like it, they can lump it . . .

It was a lovely day, a day that only May can offer. Bright, but not too hot. Nature had dressed up in her finest. The summer clothes had come out of the wardrobes, short sleeves, smelling a little of naphthalene.

They walked from Mazarita to the stadium. Mary was wearing a simple dress patterned with little spring flowers. Alekos was wearing a white linen suit. The stadium was packed: girls and boys, families with children, elderly couples—they had all taken their places in the stands and were waiting for the parade to begin.

Alekos and Mary sat down hurriedly in the first vacant seats they found. He felt that everyone was looking at them. But soon the crowd's attention turned to the parade, which was just beginning. There was applause, cheering and general rejoicing. Mothers waved proudly as they recognized their daughters sitting aloft the most beautiful carriages.

The two of them sat in silence, hardly moving, looking straight ahead.

The parade was just the beginning of the festivities—when it was over the crowds began to walk up and down the track, as if the stadium were a park. They admired the flower-decorated kiosks, bought bunches and garlands of flowers, bouquets, May-wreaths.

There was such a crowd, people were pushing, some going this way, some going that, others going in the general direction of the steps up to the Athletic Club to sit at the tables set up there, to order a soft drink, an iced coffee, an ice cream, a sorbet.

Alekos was a member of the club, a former athlete. He thought to go there and sit at one of the tables.

He felt that everyone they passed was looking at them strangely, then stopping to whisper conspiratorially. It was as if he could hear them saying, "Hey, that's Alekos, Economidis' accountant. Have you seen who he's with?" He imagined their ironic smiles, the winking, the suggestive gestures . . . the sentences left unfinished.

He met many acquaintances. Some greeted him in haste with a nod of the head, others said, "Hi, Alekos, how are you? Where are you going . . . ?" But when they saw that he was not alone, they walked on by.

A young man about Mary's age said, "Hello, Mary. How are you? What are you doing here?" They stood facing one another; they touched as the crowd continued to push forward. Then the young man realized that Mary was not alone. Alekos took her defensively by the shoulders, as if trying to protect her. A little farther on, a middle-aged man walking by himself smiled at her, and she looked away.

He must have been a friend of hers too, Alekos thought, just as he was sure that Efthimis, the bookseller, knew her. Alekos noticed out of the corner of his eye how he had stopped and turned curiously to look.

Alekos began to ask himself how many of these respectable family men, strolling with their wives and children, had crossed the *bawwaba* of the two-story *okella* in Mazarita. He began to feel that all eyes were upon him, that all the smiles and the chattering were about him. He was the target. He tried to hurry. He quickened his pace to reach the steps to the club. He felt hunted. He held out his arm, helped Mary pass in front, guided her forward to climb the few steps ahead of him. There were only three or four steps in all. He imagined that more curious eyes and ironic smiles would be awaiting them as soon as they entered the open-air terrace. He paused, he motioned to Mary to wait. He turned and looked back to the stadium. He was afraid; it was as if he were standing in front of an enormous freshly painted white wall. He stood at attention, like a condemned man, and all the Greeks of the city who had gathered in that familiar place were the firing squad. Each of them held a stone and was ready to cast it. He stood still. The crowd moved forward in silence, some with malice, others with envy, others with irony in their eyes. One by one they approached him, they took aim and cast their stone with all their strength. Powerless, defeated, Alekos looked down at the ground. He did not dare to look up. The stones flew, whistling past, left and right, but none of them found their mark, none hit him.

How long did that nightmare last? Perhaps just a second,

the blink of an eye, but that second, as in a dream, contained all the future outcries waiting to devour him, and he looked up before turning his back on the stadium.

"One of the stones will surely hit me in the face, on the head, it'll kill me," he whispered.

He closed his eyes and turned his face away, not out of fear but because he was overcome by an immense feeling of disappointment, and he asked, "Why . . .? Why . . . ?" He found the answer himself that very same evening when for hours he wandered around the poor Arab district of Anfoushi, an area he had never ventured into before.

"Because people have their own rules, their own balance, their own unwritten laws woven through time from generation to generation."

They did not sit at a table in the Athletic Club; they crossed the enclosed area and left as if they were being hunted. In silence they reached Mazarita, where Alekos left Mary, then he walked alone toward the coast. He kept walking until nightfall. He could hear the muezzin calling Allah's faithful to the last prayer of the day, while some distant chime reminded the Christians that their God cared for them too. Lost in the maze of muddy alleyways . . . he tried to get his bearings . . . he came out once more onto the coast road; he was near to Qaitbey. He climbed up onto the wall of the Corniche and sat there, not caring that he would dirty his white trousers. He looked out over the old harbor, which formed a half moon, and further on at the lights of Ramleh, which stretched out into infinity. He knew that he could not live with Mary in this city . . .

What shall I do? Should we leave, go to Athens? But how would I begin a new life in a foreign place? Of course, gradually, all the Europeans will leave Alexandria. Just as they began a century and a half ago, a mere handful of Greeks, so few will remain again . . . But even so, this is my city—I love it, it loves me. I could not imagine myself anywhere else.

There was also his mother. He had told her once that they

would have to seriously consider that one day all the Europeans would leave Alexandria.

"Our turn will come, mother," he had said.

She had looked at him obstinately, her eyes decisive, and in a tone that allowed no contradiction, she had said, "I'm not leaving here." His mother's attitude often annoyed him; either through stubbornness or pleading, she always got her own way. Just as she did in the war, when she refused to leave the city even during the heavy bombing.

"But dear Mama," he had said, "our uncles and aunts have gone, so many of our neighbors have gone, the Germans are almost outside the city. Let's go to Ismailia, to Uncle Stamatis." But she would not budge.

How long did he sit there, looking at the dark sea of the Eastern Harbor? he had lost all sense of time. He did not care about anything. He felt as if he were in a huge vacuum, alone with his doubts, the questions that plagued him, his indecision . . .

He was in a sort of trance . . . After a long while he began to feel cold—that brought him to his senses. He jumped down off the wall onto the sidewalk and slowly walked home. He lay awake all night. He smoked one cigarette after another, staring into the empty darkness.

When he felt the first rays of the sun coming in through the half-open shutters he said, relieved, "Ouf! At last, it's morning."

He left hurriedly for the office, before his mother could comment on his late return. All day he remained undecided, at that same crossroads: Mary was on one side, opposite was his mother; then there was expatriation, and facing it, the City. Which road should he take? He had not decided yet. He was postponing the inevitable "No."

He went home. As soon as Kyra Malamatenia opened the door, he knew what she was going to say. How quickly news traveled in the Great City!

"Is it true, Alekos? . . . They say that . . . "

She hesitated. Alekos did not allow her to finish the sentence. He stopped her without saying anything—he could not say a word, he simply held a finger up to his lips, and the pleading look in his eyes said, "Mama, say nothing . . . hush."

Things ended there just like that, without his making any decisions. There was no need for him to say much to Mary; there was almost nothing he could say, in fact. A few months later she left for Athens. Why didn't she try? Why didn't she weep? Why did she submit to her fate? Why didn't she help him . . . ?

A year passed, and a second, and then another. Almost all the Europeans left the city, and his mother departed on that journey that allows no contradiction.

Often at night he would have the same dream, over and over. He had died. He saw his body lying completely still, wrapped in a white shroud, and he was looking on from the shade of a date palm.

Curious, he waited to see what would happen to the body from which he had been separated. It should have been taken to the cemetery, but all the Greeks of the city had left, and along with them the deacons, the priests, and Archimandrite Karaminas. Who would give his body the Christian burial it deserved? There was nobody there; he was the last Greek in the city.

He looked uneasily around to see what would become of his earthly double . . .

Suddenly, the Egyptians undertook to bury him. Four of them came, picked him up, and carried him on their shoulders.

"Ah!" he cried in surprise. He recognized them: it was Lutfi the coffeehouse keeper, Ahmad the tobacconist, Mursi the carter, and Musa the office boy, and a great crowd followed, all locals. And he walked among them. They were all shouting with one voice, rhythmically, loudly, as if trying to wake him up. *"La ilaha illa Allah! Muhammad rasul Allah!"*

(There is no god but Allah! Muhammad is the Prophet of Allah!)

They chanted the same declaration of faith over and over again, while they held his body up high above their heads like a banner at a demonstration. When the cortege had passed Pompey's Pillar and was approaching the ruined Arab tombs, then he woke up . . .

•

Alekos began to gather up his things. He closed the umbrella and got ready to leave. Today's trip to the beach was over. Another Sunday had passed. He took one last look at the sea. For a moment his heart leapt. He felt that there might still be some ray of hope left for him. Like the last temptation, it crossed his mind that he might go beyond the sea . . . But then he remembered the words of the poet, which had been hovering in his brain for a long time:

> *You will find no new lands, you will find no other seas.*
> *The city will follow you. You will roam the same streets.*
> *And you will grow old in the same neighborhoods;*
> *And you will grow gray in these same houses.*
> *You will always come back to this city. For another land —*
> *do not hope —*
> *There is no ship for you, there is no road.*
> *As you have ruined your life here*
> *In this tiny corner, so you have ruined it the world over.*

Were those words written for me? How apt they are!
"No," he said. "Never mind . . . It's too late."

The engine of the tired old Citroën chugged and coughed, started reluctantly, lazily kicking up a cloud of dust, while a flock of quails, perhaps the last of the year, passed hurriedly overhead and disappeared on their interminable path to the south.

Glossary

Fr = French; Ar = Arabic; Gr = Greek; It = Italian

abri: (Fr) air-raid shelter

bawwab: (Ar) doorkeeper, janitor.

bawwaba: (Ar) entrance to a building, or the small room, generally located under the stairwell, where the *bawwab* and his family live

Cape Tenaron: the southernmost point of the Greek main land; in antiquity there was a sanctuary and an oracle of Poseidon here, which was also a refuge for pirates

Chios: the Greek island of Chios was a Genoese posses sion from 1307 to 1566; an inhabitant of the island is known as a Chiot

Copt: an Egyptian Christian of the Coptic Orthodox Church

Corniche: (Fr) the coast road in Alexandria

Eunostos: ancient Alexandria had two harbors, the Eunostos, or the Port of Good Return, and the Megas Limin, the eastern harbor

ezba: (Ar) private agricultural estate in rural Egypt

Fayoum: oasis south of Cairo with extensive late Roman and early Christian burials, in which a painted portrait on wood of the deceased person was usually placed over the face of the mummified body; these portraits of men and women are characterized by large, well-defined, black eyes

fellah: (Ar) peasant farmer of Egypt (plural *fellahin*)

foustanella: (Gr) sort of traditional kilt worn by Greek shepherds

full: (Ar) local variety of jasmine

fuul: (Ar) baked fava beans, a staple of the Egyptian diet

gallabiya: (Ar) long tunic traditionally worn by Egyptian men

kavassis: (Gr) consular guard (from the Arabic *qawwas*)

khamsin: (Ar) hot, sand-laden wind that blows in Egypt in spring

Kyra: (Gr) term of address to an elderly country woman

Kyria: (Gr) term of address to a city woman

milaya: (Ar) black wrap worn by Egyptian women in traditional quarters

NAAFI: Navy, Army, and Air Force Institute, which supplied the British armed forces with tinned foods, cigarettes, and other provisions

okella: (Gr) building of two or three floors with one or two apartments on each floor (from the Arabic *wikala*)

the poet: Constantine Cavafy (1863–1933)

sa'idi: (Ar) an Upper Egyptian

Shami: (Ar) a Christian Syrian

Shamm al-Nesim: (Ar) the Egyptian spring festival, on the Monday following Orthodox Easter

shawish: (Ar) Egyptian police constable

shisha: (Ar) water-pipe for smoking flavored tobacco

Spyros Louis: Greek shepherd who, without any athletic training, won the marathon at the first modern Olympic Games, held in Athens in 1896, and became a legend in his lifetime

Tsirigo: another name for the island of Kithira

zibib: (Ar) a Greek and Levantine anisette